Jack & Evan

In Verse

Aaron Hundley

FIRST EDITION

ISBN 979-8-218-64579-3

www.aaronhundley.com

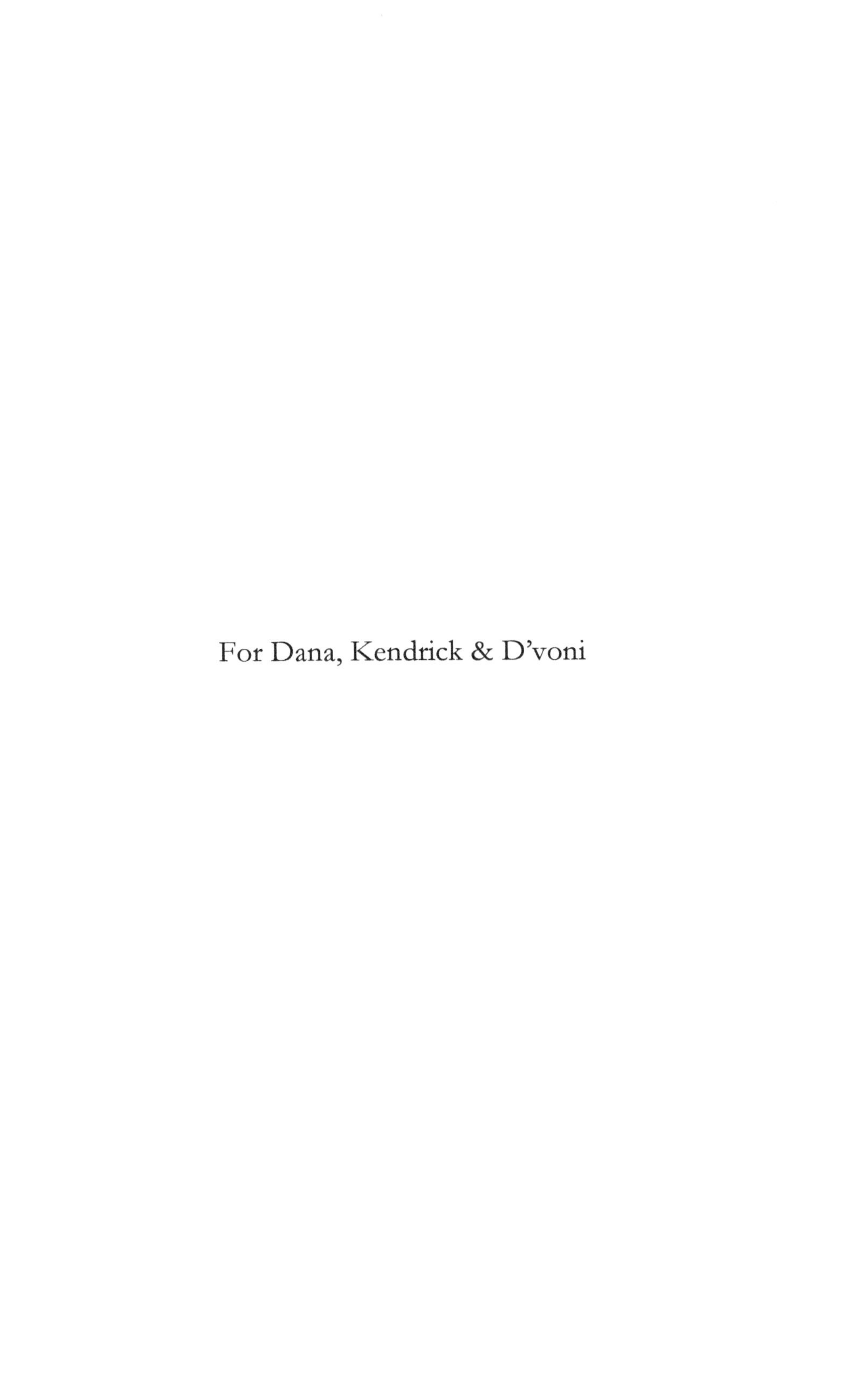

For Dana, Kendrick & D'voni

Jack & Evan

FADE IN:

EXT. THERAPIST'S OFFICE — DAY — JANUARY 2015

A small brick building sits on a charming side street, somewhere in Northern California. The camera swoops up a hilly street through a brownstone window.

INT. THERAPIST'S OFFICE

Inside, the rented office space contains an oatmeal-colored armchair, a wooden bookshelf, one round end table holding a black-potted peace lily, a lamp, and a psychotherapist whose black-framed MFT degree from Cal State East Bay hangs on the wall behind the therapist. The room is dominated by one green leather couch, which holds one of our main characters, Evan Harris 6'0-6'1", slender, lean, dark brown complexion, low top fade, new beard, neat but patchy. The therapist can only be seen from the back.

THERAPIST:

Well, I think the best way to do this is to reach out to Jack. And let's talk about it at our next session in two weeks.

EVAN:

What do you want me to say?

THERAPIST:

What would you like to say?

EVAN:

I don't know.

THERAPIST:

Do you not know what to say? Or are you afraid he is not going to respond?

EVAN:

Both.

THERAPIST:

You mentioned you guys used to write to each other as kids. Maybe you'd be more comfortable writing to him?

EVAN:

I don't know.

THERAPIST:

Ok, well, maybe send a text or leave a voice message or whatever you feel comfortable with. Can you do that?

EVAN:

…Yeah.

THERAPIST:

Great, I will see you in two weeks.

SUBTITLE: THE NEXT DAY.

Close up of only Evan's hands as they type out a text. He is holding his phone over a peanut butter sandwich in what is presumably his neat, spare kitchen.

EVAN:

Yo, Jack, what up? This is Evan, how you been?

SUBTITLE: FOUR DAYS LATER.

Close up on thumbs, though we can see that Evan is in the driver's seat in a car.

EVAN:

I just wanted to check up on you. Everything good?

SUBTITLE: A WEEK AND A HALF LATER.

Again, close up on Evan's hands texting, this time on a park bench.

EVAN:

Well, I hope all is good with you. I would love to catch up. My bad for being so distant these past years.

INT. THERAPIST'S OFFICE — DAY

Evan is seated on the same green couch.

THERAPIST:

Do you plan to keep trying to reach him?

EVAN:

I don't know, I just don't want to be too forceful.

THERAPIST:

Ok, that's fair, Evan. Do whatever feels good for you.

EVAN:

Ok.

THERAPIST:

So, what else would you like to work on today?

EVAN:

…but what if he never responds?

THERAPIST:

(Sighing.) It's scary to make ourselves vulnerable to rejection. But to respond to your question, I would ask you, what if he does? And if he does, doesn't it seem like some honest communication between you two could be healing?

EVAN:

Yeah.

EVAN'S BEDROOM — NIGHT

Evan lies spread across his queen-size bed on his gray duvet cover surrounded by two white and gold nightstands. The nightstand to the right holds a white digital clock showing the time, 10:20. We only see the conversation from Evan's point of view.

EVAN TEXTS:

Are you mad at me?

The clock clicks over to 10:25, and a text appears on Evan's phone.

Yes.

EVAN TEXTS:

I have my ideas why, but I don't want to put words in your mouth. Can you tell me?

Nah, I don't want to talk to you.

EVAN TEXTS:

I am sorry for everything. I never knew it would turn out this way.

Yes, you did, and that's what you wanted. So now I got nothing else to say to you.

The clock shows 10:35.

EVAN TEXTS:

I am really sorry.

SUBTITLE: TWO DAYS LATER.

Evan sits in a restaurant booth texting.

EVAN TEXTS:

Do you remember we used to write to each other?

SUBTITLE: 15 MINUTES LATER.

Camera is tight on phone screen.

EVAN TEXTS:

That was fun, huh?

Looking at it now, I think it was our way of expressing things we couldn't say—or at least that is the case for me.

> I know you don't want to talk to me, so I won't keep bothering you. I just want to say that I wish at times we could go back to that.

Why did you stop then? And why the hell are you saying all of this now?

EVAN TEXTS:

> I am trying to make sense out of all of this, too. Been seeing a therapist for a while now. But all of a sudden, what has happened with us has been hitting me hard.

> But there is more to this answer and I would like to answer it the best way I can. Do you mind if I try?

> I understand if you don't want to reply.

Evan writes and discards several essays, then decides he needs to boil his message down to its barest essence. He emails the following.

To: Jackson (1)

Black yoga pants, warmed lattes,

preferred Sunday morning aesthetic

in the district.

I had Tony visiting me—

and if my faded sweatpants

and his musty tee didn't make us

outsiders, certainly

our dark skin did.

What was I doing there?

I asked myself this question often—

but that day the more

literal answer was simpler:

We were on a walk

to find food.

Above us,

not the typical

overcast skies

of the city—

but a haze

that hinted at

distant fires.

We settled

on an out-of-place

donut shop

where I got

my usual

maple bar,

no filling.

Possibly because

the older Korean lady

always added

free donut holes

in my bag.

More likely

because

the out-of-place

found one

another.

My younger

brother called,

asked if I had heard

from mama.

I hadn't.

He mentioned

he couldn't reach her,

which was rare.

So we agreed

to hang up. I said I'd

try my luck calling her,

he'd call our older brother

who lived a five-minute freeway drive

from her side of town.

Each of my four attempts

went straight

to my mama's

voicemail.

The haze around me

no longer seemed

due to distant fires.

Tony's voice

grew muffled.

With less oxygen

than before,

our steps slowed.

Eventually,

my phone rang.

My younger brother again.

"Hello?"

"Get over to mama's house now!"

"What's going on?" I asked.

"Her car is out front, the doors are

locked, and nobody is answering."

Tony drove in silence.

I spoke non-stop out

of discomfort.

We passed

the toll booths,

the golden bridge,

descended into

Marin County.

My phone rang.

This time

my sister.

"Hello?"

"Hello? Evan?"

"Yeah, I'm here…."

My sister sobbing.

"WHAT'S GOING ON?" I asked.

"SHE'S DEAD!"

INT. THERAPIST'S OFFICE — DAY — FEBRUARY 2015

EVAN:

I am not going to send him any more messages.

THERAPIST:

I understand, but are you going to stop writing?

EVAN:

I don't know, probably.

THERAPIST:

How did it feel to write it?

EVAN:

It was hard…but good.

THERAPIST:

Well, why not keep writing? Do you have more to say?

EVAN:

I definitely have more to say, but I'll be honest. I texted Jack and said it's ok if he doesn't respond, but I really hope he does.

THERAPIST:

Then why not keep writing him?

EVAN:

Because he's not trying to hear from me.

THERAPIST:

But he did ask you a question, right?

EVAN:

Yeah.

THERAPIST:

So what if your past email was just your first response? And you didn't want to send it all in one email? We are talking about a lot of history between you two and many years of catching up.

EVAN:

Do you mind if I continue to share what I wrote with you?

THERAPIST:

I don't mind at all.

EVAN:

Ok, thanks. I want to make sure I am not trying to overly
explain myself, you know?

THERAPIST:

I do. So then don't explain, express.

Evan sends another email.

To: Jackson (2)

Your silence had me wondering

if I appropriately answered

your question of "why now?"

Certainly, that tragic moment
was the impetus.

I can't deny the origin.

We lived in a strange part of town as kids.

The roach-infested, Section 8 apartments

were hard enough, but life twisted the knife

having us surrounded by suburbia.

Because we weren't in the South Side,
my complaints about
our North Side dwellings felt trivial.

But I wanted out.

I remember a summer night

sitting in my room, eyes closed,
fingers crossed, praying

to leave this place

after watching Pablo's mom
from Apartment 12
be knocked unconscious
by her boyfriend.

I was a shivering nine-year-old,

yet still questioned my courage

when the man walked past me,
unthreatened by my witnessing,

as if I were invisible.

I always knew you wanted out, too.

You wrote about it,

but never acted

as if you did.

Around others

you faced danger by kicking
at the dirt beneath you,

puffing your chest,
letting me only see
your softer side through your writings.

We and our poor Mexican neighbors

were forced to find our way
around the well-to-do white folks.

I kept focus on getting out
by watching my mama.

She had been sober
for most of the life I can remember—

another reason complaining about

our living conditions felt trivial.

Escaping the South Side

kept her clean.

My siblings and I were her motivation.
Seeing that work for her,

I made my younger brother and cousins

my motivation.

Her strength was crucial for our family,

but she couldn't fill the missing link
of a positive male role model.

My dad was only his whole, healthy self
when Mama threatened to kick him out.

Their fights, his off-and-on drug use,

was like waiting for an aftershock
following a quake.

My older brother and sister

had it worse, the mist

encircling their memories

not as thick.

Yet, with all that,

we did make do
with what we were dealt.

I remember full sprints
home from the blacktop
when the ice cream truck serenaded.

When raiding our house

like the FBI in search

of dimes and nickels

took so long, we were left

chasing the truck
waving our fists full of coins.

Our sugar cravings then

had to be satisfied by

10-cent, cherry-flavored

Airheads, Jolly Ranchers,

or Laffy-Taffy at 7-11.

If it was too late for
the walk to the store,

we would settle

for off-brand cereal

hoping my siblings
hadn't left the bag open

for the roaches

to dine in that night.

From: Jackson (3)

Trese told me

that my first

word was "No."

> *That I walked*
>
> *around repeating*
>
> *it, to hear*
>
> *myself say it.*

> *As if I intuitively knew,*
>
> *one day I would need it.*

When I was

four years old,

she started seeing

a man from the South Side.

One day I said,

"He make

me fall down."

The next time he came over,
she left the room, but

peeked around the corner—

and sure enough,

that bastard stuck

his foot out
as I toddled by.

She came
from around

the corner

to protect me,

but I'd already

planted my baby teeth
into his leg.

That was the last of him.

Trese always said
I just knew things.

But situations like that

also wised me up.

> *When I wasn't with*
>
> *my big cousin Marcel,*
>
> *I was with you.*

> > *The summer*
> >
> > *we were ten,*
> >
> > *I smoked weed*
> > *for the first time*
> > *down by the river*
> >
> > *with Marcel.*

By the afternoon,

me and you

got to show off

the perfect chemistry

we had on the basketball

court we created by

cutting the bottom out

of an old milk crate.

> *Together, we dreamed*
>
> *out loud.*

Pretending

we were star basketball

players from

the '90s.

We had

many things

in common.

Mainly because

outside of family,

we were only

one of the few
black people
on the North Side.

Though, what

brought us

closer was

our love for

words.

How did that

change?

Why did we
have to keep that

to ourselves?

At times, I

found myself infatuated
by the world
inside the complex.

Drugs, violence—

the life of a villain.

It was that side of

me that scared

you away.

I wonder

how you appeared

to look down on me

when we stood at

the same level.

I'd moved from L.A.,
other end of the state,

where my gang-affiliated

aunties and uncles lived—

and first ended up

on the South Side

before moving to

the North.

Together, we were

never bored.

Exploring the river
below the complex,

which collided with
the salt water of the bay.

We tore up
the forest,

using bamboo sticks

to rip through

unforgiving

blackberry bushes,

pretending to be
researching Bengal tigers.

Or we followed yo'

younger brother

to find obsidians,

sharpening them

on a boulder,

tying the stones to

our sticks to make

unsuccessful

spear-fishing attempts

during low tides.

We had all the freedom, but

you always knew

when we traveled too far.

Marcel,
four years older—
moved from L.A., too—

always wanted to
start his own gang,

took me along

as we circled

the neighborhood

for kids to recruit,
then to a corner store

to shoulder-tap winos

or steal 40s to get drunk
behind South Side High.

He had me fight
some of the kids to prove
they could hold their own,
which I did without complaint.

I didn't enjoy it.

Until they hit me first.

When I tasted

my blood—

I wanted theirs.

INT. THERAPIST'S OFFICE – DAY – MID-FEBRUARY 2015

EVAN:

Do you think he ended it abruptly?

THERAPIST:

No, to me, it just seems like he's keeping the door open.

EVAN:

Maybe. I'm surprised he had that much to say.

THERAPIST:

How does that make you feel?

EVAN:

Both sad and good.

THERAPIST:

Are you comfortable with continuing your interaction?

EVAN:

Yeah, I'm scared to be honest, but curious where it all goes.

Evan drafts his response that night.

I appreciate

your response.

I found myself

getting defensive.

Typing and deleting

words to refute

the notion I looked

down on you.

I thought:

"You were my

best friend,

how could that
be possible?"

But then a

memory dropped.

It's amazing

how writing

you has made

me recall things

I hadn't thought

of in years,

even purposely

forgot.

I am embarrassed

to admit how

many drafts
it has taken me
to write this short

response.

But I am far

more ashamed

about this memory.

Do you recall

a time when you first felt
I pulled away?

SUBTITLE: THE NEXT DAY...

From: Jackson (5)

I was at my

auntie's in the

South Side
visiting Marcel.

We met up with

one of his homeboys, D,
a tall cat
with twisted teeth,

smoky black skin,
and a high-top fade.

We stood behind

South Side High

in a back alley

we used to tag
with stolen spray paint.

Marcel and D

paid me no attention

after cutting me off
from their joint
for "coughing too much."

I said I'd meet them
at the basketball court

just above us.

To get there,

I had to walk
up a small path

covered by
towering trees

and dried brush.

Wrappers and liquor bottles
littered the path
as I walked slowly, watching

my step, hoping the stench
of old urine would subside.

Just off the path,
I came across
a discarded

black revolver.

I put the ball

between my legs,

                              picked up the gun,

                              aimed toward

                              the ground,

                              squeezed the trigger

                              multiple times,

                              but nothing happened.

I thought to

put it back, but

then remembered

the week before when

a group of boys waited

for me and Marcel outside

a movie theatre.

                    I was scared, and

               the only one to protect me,
               Marcel, was scared too.

                              I slipped the gun

                              into my hoodie pocket,

                              continued

                              toward the court,
                              past the baseball fields.

At the courts,
a group of older boys
played on one half.

I took the revolver
out of my pocket,

slipped it under a pile a leaves

where the grass

became the blacktop.

I dribbled Marcel's

dusty ball,

started to shoot

on the vacant half

of the court.

One of the boys said,

"Hey, we about to
play full court."

I got my rebound

and stared
at the boys, saw

some laughing,

one's eyes daring

me to respond.

I walked over

to the pile of leaves,

replaced the ball

with the revolver,

walked back

toward the boys

and waved the gun until

they scattered off

like roaches.

I was afraid of how much
I enjoyed that power—

so I ran off myself,

found the nearest bush
and dumped the weapon.

Those boys never

came back to

the court—

and I never told
Marcel.

I never told

anyone.

If it ever

got out,

I would have

been sent away.

But from that day,

I was afraid

those guys would learn
I was connected

to Marcel and retaliate.

But of course, this

was not what

you asked me.

I will tell you about that.

We got hungry after

ten minutes of playing,

so we left.

We headed towards

Food 4 Less, skipping
the fried bologna sandwiches

at my auntie's for bigger prizes

like Moon Pies,

Starbursts,
every kind of soda.

We'd had plenty of success
pocketing these items before.

"We can see what we got
at my house," D suggested.

"Nah, lets just go up here," Marcel demanded.

I nodded my head in agreement.

"Y'all go ahead,
somebody in here
might know my mama,"

D said, stopping
before the parking lot.

"Man, stop trippin',
ain't nobody
gon' see you," Marcel said.

"Naw, man, go on,
I ain't goin' in there.
I'll get up with y'all later," D insisted.

"Yeah ok,
you a bitch then,"
Marcel shouted.

I didn't believe D heard

for on the South Side
those words

required a fight.

That day

the wind was

heavy off the bay,
skimming the water and
numbing the little fingers

I needed for thievery.

Inside resembled nothing

different than before.

So I tried to rely on our

tactics of the past.

Split up, get what we

liked, and meet out front.

Maybe D's worry
spooked me,

but whatever

it was, I knew

something was off.

Instead of

stuffing my pockets,

I grabbed one pack of

Starburst,

circled the store,

headed up front
to see Marcel

heading out as well,

with practiced composure.

Once out,
we kept a slow pace
to not tip anyone off.

Then I remembered

another instruction.

When the light concrete

of the pathway meets

the parking lot blacktop,

run.

We were

two steps away

before

we heard,

"You two need to come with me."

We entered the store.

Ages were lied about.

Auntie was called,

Trese drove across

town to come get me.

42

SUBTITLE: THAT SAME NIGHT

To: Jackson (6)

Word traveled fast

in the complex.

I sat on the top

bunk bed
(shared with my

younger brother

to make space for

my older brother's

twin bed).

My mama, my dad,
and my younger brother

(who hid behind them)

stood outside

our bedroom door
like it was an

intervention.

"What gang is Jack in?" my mama asked.

I knew you weren't

really in one, but

that you were

interested, so

I just shrugged.

I was taken aback

by how she dragged

my dad into this;
he stood there

with his head down.

I must admit,
in that moment,

I could see why a kid

would get
in trouble

if that meant
he'd also get

his father's attention.

"Well, he just got caught stealing with his cousin Marcel,
and if that

boy keeps it up, I am telling you, he's gon' end up dead or
in jail," Mama went on.

I nodded,

waiting for

her to explain

how what

happened with

you would affect me.

"Meet me in my room, I want to show you something,"
she said.

That night she showed me

the movie

Menace II Society.

All of it, from the drug dealing

to the main character
gunned down
just as he was trying

to leave that life behind.

It was based in L.A.,
which made me
think of you.

It was a lot

for an elementary

school kid, but

so were our lives.

She then played

Boomerang, starring

Eddie Murphy,
to give me a visual

of a successful black man.

"Now, which one do you want to be?"
she asked me when it ended.

I remember a

big pause.

Maybe I am making it
more dramatic

than it was in real time,
but dramatic is how it felt
for this was the moment

that begin to shift

our friendship.

"I want to be like Eddie Murphy."

"Ok, well, you have to watch who you hang with.
Just because we live in these apartments,
don't mean these are the only friends you need to have,"
she said.

I agreed.

Before then,

I had dreams.

But from that night on,
taking control of my life
became a real practice.

From: Jackson (7)

Days after

being caught stealing,
my auntie, Marcel's mama,
was beaten into a coma
by her new husband.

He bit a piece of her ear off,

knocked her out,
left her bleeding.

I already did not fit in

at North Hills Elementary,

but between

the new distance

from you and that

news, I started fighting

in school almost every day.

Our teacher

Mr. Lombard

called Trese

at home.

She was on the couch,

legs crossed, house phone

pressed to her ear
when I walked in.

My lungs were oppressed,

as usual, by the burning cigarette
resting between her fingers.

"I don't know what it is,"
she said through a sigh.

"I think he is sad about my sister,
but he won't talk about it when I ask him."

She was right.

I didn't even

write and

share it

with you.

But it was more

than my auntie.

It was the weight

of my family's pain

pushing down

on my shoulders.

From the pain
of Trese's oldest sister

killed by a violent man
before I was born to now.

My aunties and uncles

confronted their pain
with dance and laughter

during family celebrations
until the trick wore off

and darkened clouds

began to hover—

which sent them

on another run

to the liquor store.

Months after

I got caught stealing,

North Hills Elementary

had their annual spring barbecue,

when parents could enjoy
a cheeseburger with their kids
on their lunch breaks.

> *The school asked*
>
> *parents to pay*
>
> *for the meal,*
>
> *so that meant*
>
> *I was stuck*
>
> *with my usual*
>
> *school-paid,*
> *packaged*
>
> *bean burrito.*

> > *I hadn't even*
> >
> > *asked Trese,*
> >
> > *always cognizant*
> >
> > *of the multiple*
> >
> > *jobs she held down,*
> >
> > *leaving her*

no extra

cash or time.

But as a kid,

it's hard to see
what you can't have

when everyone around you
seems to have it.

I guess

that doesn't

change.

Carrying my lunch tray
searching for a place to eat,
I looked, but,
couldn't find you,

so went searching
for a quiet place
to be alone.

To do that,

I had to walk

through a sea full

of North Side's

white families,

enjoying their

lunches on the lawn.

I was stopped

when I heard

"Hey, you that kid that keeps picking on my son?"

It was Jeffrey Hall's

father. A stalky,

clean-shaven man

with a smile I knew

even then had gotten him

out of jams someone like me
could never hope
to grin my way past.

I knew this because

Jeffrey had inherited

the same smile and

received a tap
on the wrist after

he embarrassed me
by saying I looked
like O.J. Simpson
before running away.

"Yeah, I heard you are picking on my son too," said some lady with
ear length hair and a brown freckled nose.

Trese was always

saving me

from being

expelled.

Leaving work
the second

she got the call

from the principal.

Making sure

all sides were told.
Putting me

on punishment

at home for
the part I played.

"You better leave our son alone, He's got a black belt,"
a third woman joined in.

I said nothing.

Though, I wanted to

tell Jeffrey's dad
his son was no angel.

Tell him how Jeffrey
gathered a group of boys
to circle me at recess

and mock my baggy pants,

my dirty shoes,
my black skin.

How he stood back,
laughing

at this "wild animal"
charging his cronies.

I wanted to

tell all the parents
how a grown man

drove past me,
shouted "nigger"
out his window
as I biked alone

days before.

I wanted to tell them

my struggles at home,

say I was sorry

I'd punched

some of their kids.

I wanted to tell them

harassing me, or making me sit
in Principal Murphy's office,
did nothing to help.

What I really

wanted was a hug.

But instead,

I walked on,

sat at an empty bench,

slightly hidden behind
well-groomed bushes.

Sat and ate my burrito,

and watched our classmates

finish their lunches and

head to the playground

to show their parents
some of their new tricks

on the monkey bars.

INT. THERAPIST'S OFFICE — DAY — LATE FEBRUARY 2015

Evan is sitting on his regular couch, but his hair is unusually unkempt.

THERAPIST:

Seems like communicating with Jack is helping you remember a lot more about your childhood.

EVAN:

Yeah, I felt awful reading that about him being alone. I should have been there with him.

THERAPIST:

(Sighing) That was hard to read, but Evan, I wanted to check in with you. How are you dealing with this while grieving your mom?

EVAN:

Oh, well, it's been only what? Almost two years? I don't think it takes me away from grieving her. Actually, going this deep with Jack feels harder at times than my loss.

THERAPIST:

Expand on that.

EVAN:

I definitely cried more after my mama passed. There was more of a shock. But in my experience, guys don't really communicate like this, you know? I know me and Jack kind of did as kids, but he was right. Even then I was always wary of how it would look. That's why I told him to get rid of what we wrote. My brothers would have blasted me if they found it.

THERAPIST:

Do you still want to continue talking to Jack?

EVAN:

Yeah, but I am torn. Because I know how I treated him only gets worse, and how many times can I say sorry before I start annoying him? I also have some fun memories that I am starting to remember, but I don't want to try to seem as if I am diminishing his pain by sharing that.

THERAPIST:

Do they involve him?

EVAN:

Some of them, but some don't.

THERAPIST:

I get the feeling Jack is the type of person that just wants
you to honestly express yourself, so why not write what
you want to write and just see where that leads you?

Evan sends another email.

To: Jackson (8)

Interesting

you brought up

Jeffrey Hall because

when I think about

how my life has gone,

his small role had

a positive impact.

I agree, he

wasn't always

that kind, and

it didn't help that

he was this tall,

preppy kid with a

comb-over and a

prominent nose

that seemed

to sniff at everything

he considered

beneath him.

But I had

his respect.

He could tell

I found some

of his prankster

tendencies humorous.

Which really meant

I was infatuated with

the promise of freedom

I felt with him,

knowing we could

slip out of paying

for the trouble

we caused.

He also respected

my athletic prowess,

first apparent

one day in sixth grade

when Mr. Andersen

approached me with Jeffrey

and remember Su Starks?

He asked if I wanted to run

in this annual track meet

for all the elementary schools.

I had never heard of it.

As far as I knew,

my older siblings

had never done it.

"It's Saturday," Mr. Andersen said,

"and if you can get your younger brother

to run with us, we will have

the four fastest kids in our school

on the relay team."

"Hey, um, my mom

can pick you and your brother up

and drop you off, too,"

Jeffrey chimed in,

letting me know he wanted me

to say yes.

I knew if I did it,

my younger brother

would, so I agreed.

We practiced

during lunch recess,

running fast,

exchanging a green

aluminum baton.

On the day

of the race,

my mama

was at work

by the time

Jeffrey's mom

drove into the

complex.

I pretended I didn't see

the dirty diapers

and trash on the ground

in hopes they didn't either.

Pulling up

to our future

middle school,

I could see the morning fog

had overstayed its welcome

as fallen dead leaves

held a race of their own,

powered by a cold wind

that bit into

my excitement.

We met

Mr. Anderson

on the track,

his tall lanky body

in a track suit,

unfazed by the wind.

"You guys ready to run?" he greeted us

with uncustomary cheer.

"Su is warmed up

and over at the bleachers

with her dad," Mr. Andersen went on.

I could see her short, straight

black hair easily

as she was

the only brown

girl in that section.

I then glanced

at my and my brother's

"athletic wear":

black FILA shoes

a size too big;

sweatpants;

a plain, black

oversized t-shirt

with

bleach stains

that looked like

a modern-art design.

"I already told Su,"

Mr. Anderson said,

"but I switched some things up.

Jeffrey, you will lead,

then hand it to Su—"

He turned to me and my brother.

"—now here's where I need your help.

Which one of you

wants to bring the race home?"

My brother,

always eager

to beat me,

got his hand

up the quickest.

"Ok, that means Su

will hand it to you next, Evan—"

he said before checking his watch.

"We have a couple of minutes.

I am going to get Su

so we can practice a little more."

As we waited,

I watched

other schools

practice what

I found out

later was called

the 4x100 relay.

Jeffrey's mom

bent down to tie

my brother's ratty

shoelaces.

Minutes passed.

The small bleachers

packed with families.

The fog remained.

The wind died.

And before my nerves

could take over,

we were all lined up

in our places.

Bang!

Jeffrey jumped

out to a good start,

but was

neck and neck

with a boy

with a high-top fade,

and all new gear.

Bending the

corner, he

extended the baton

as Su started to

pick up speed.

But just as

he released

his grip, the

baton dropped.

I could see my breath

while watching Su

swoop it up

and dart off

with two other

schools now in

the lead.

Within a few strides,

she caught one, then worked

to catch the leader.

With less than 50 meters

to go, Su hit another gear,

blowing past the frontrunner,

leaving me in great shape

as I took the baton,

sprinting as if

no one was watching.

Without a threat,

I had time to glance

at my brother's opponents.

My brother was the smallest kid

in the race.

Standing next to him

was the biggest,

a man-boy who somehow

already had

thick black sideburns

and a thin mustache.

As I made

the final exchange

I said a tiny prayer:

if we don't win,

at least don't let

this giant

eat my brother.

My brother's

turn over

was too fast

and his shoes too big,

causing him to stumble.

Though we had

a big lead, his trip

gave the giant

a chance.

At the midpoint,

he was on

my brother's

heels. Through

sheer terror,

just like Su,

he found

another gear.

Raw instinct

took over,

driving him

over the finish line

into the open arms

of an ecstatic

Mr. Anderson.

Pats on our backs,

cheers from the small crowd

of strangers,

changed our lives

that day.

As did the conversation

on our way home

with Jeffrey's mom.

"Evan, Jeffrey always talks about

how fast you are. Now I see why.

Have you ever thought about

trying out for the Falcons

football team?" she asked.

"No, I haven't," I replied.

"Well, you should think about it.

You guys would be good."

My thought in that moment

makes me think

of you, Jack.

How you mentioned

that you didn't

want to ask your

mama for money.

I could just hear

my mama saying,

"Ev, now you know

I ain't got no football money—"

as I had heard her say

to my older brother.

But I wasn't going to say

this to Jeffrey's mom.

"I can ask my mom when she gets home.

Thank you for the ride," I said.

Me and my brother hopped out

to return to our life in the complex.

Evan sits alone on his bed opening another email.

From: Jackson (9)

I used mayonnaise

to get old chewing gum

out of our brown carpet.

> *Soap and water*
>
> *to clean*
>
> *emptied cabinets,*
>
> *flushing out*
>
> *cockroach eggs.*

> *It happened*
>
> *so fast.*

Trese grew tired

of going up

to the school

after I got into

squabbles.

> *She knew*
> *I was not innocent,*
>
> *but also knew*
>
> *North Hill Elementary*

was ill-equipped
to care for a black boy
from our environment.

I remember

her telling

Principal Murphy,

"I moved here

because I wanted

my son to go to safe schools,
and this school is safe,
I just don't know

how safe it is for him."

We were on our way

out of town.

Trese had found
steady work, come

across a house

twenty miles south.

I dreamed of
her descriptions of

the lemon-tree

in our front yard,

the big backyard.

I hadn't gone

to see the place;
her description

was enough to

paint it real.

I did know the

neighborhood

was new, cheap, friendly

Section 8 housing.

While cleaning,

I remember

wondering
if I would miss

the cockroaches.

Stomping them
provided some release
for built-up tension.

But mostly

while cleaning,

I dreamt of

my future

adventures.

I imagined

you visiting

all the time,

figuring me
living in a nice house
would show you

I'm safe to
hang out with.

Weeks before

I was on the hunt,
treating empty boxes

like money.

My effort

got us boxes

stacked to the ceiling.

Yet before

leaving, there

were still a

couple of things

needed to

be handled.

One, was to head down

to the river with you
one last time.

Two, and it had to

happen in the

final moments—

when the U haul

was packed

and running,

to punch Marco,

for stealing yo'

bike the year before.

We never reached

that day, though.

The day before

moving day,

Trese came

to me and said,
"I have to file

for bankruptcy."

"What is that?" I asked.

"It means I co-signed for a car
fo' yo' auntie, but she ain't been paying

her car notes, so now I'm

stuck with payments I can't afford,"
she answered bluntly.

All of which meant
nothing to
an eleven-year-old.

And she knew it,
so she simplified,

"My credit is to'e up now,
so we can't move into the house."

The tower of

boxes were

taken down
over the
next month.

Fortunately, our

landlord liked

Trese because

she never missed

payments,

so he allowed us

to stay put

even after we'd given

our thirty days notice.

Over the next year,

what kept me and you

around one another
was our friendship

with Roger.

You and Roger

had football

in common.

Me and Roger

talked about

what we thought

we knew about

girls and hip hop.

I basically

regurgitated what I heard
from Marcel or older cats

around the complex.

Roger lived
in one of the few

pockets of the North Side
with some tough

white kids.

His parents were

lenient with his

curfew and friend

selection,

which led to

older boys

organizing fistfights

between him and

other kids

at the creek

near his house.

With Roger's slicked

back hair,

Dickies pants,

scarlet and gold

49er jacket,

black and white

Nike Cortez

shoes.

—plus his 25 percent

Peruvian genes

presenting themselves

in the summers—

    he ran into

    trouble with

    Mexican gang members
    mistaking him for a rival.

        We had kindergarten together.
         Then in second grade,
          I got in a fight with
         a kid by the slide and Roger
         stepped in on the kid's behalf.
          So I socked him, too.

After that,

he watched

me with

a vengeful

squint.

    The tension

    led to our own
     little crews
     getting into a

sandbox squabble.
This ended in fifth grade
when I heard him rapping

Tupac.

I will never

forget his round

face, body like

a small hibernating bear.

It was

strange to see
a white kid

walk with our

hitch in his step.

We blended
our crews, but

had no rivals.,
just pretended.

We recruited

kids in the

complex,

even yo'

younger brother,

which I know

you hated.

> *We made him fight*
> *for his ranking*
> *in the crew—*

> *and come along*

> *on our trips*

> *to steal deli sandwiches,*
> *tips, bikes left on*

> *front lawns, pizza*

> *from delivery boys.*

Me, you, and

yo' younger brother
used to meet Roger

at the halfway point
in the industrial area,
between his home and ours.

> *Right in front*

> *of where yo' mama*

> *took us*

> *to trade in*

all the cans we collected,
crushed and bagged
for a few extra dollars.

Our life of crime
included wholesome activities, too.
We would walk to a field

near the meeting point

to play football.

Until we got hungry.

Not having money

most of the time,

me, Roger, and yo'

younger brother
would head out
on a mission

to change that.

It's funny

how you

never wanted

any part of

it until yo'

stomach started

to growl.

INT. THERAPIST'S OFFICE — DAY — EARLY MARCH 2015

Evan is taking his usual seat. He's wearing faded sweats and a wrinkled T-shirt, and his hair is even more unkempt than the last time we saw him.

EVAN:

For me, it's not necessarily the holidays or anniversaries. I can feel sad about it anytime.

THERAPIST:

Absolutely, these things come in waves.

EVAN:

But of course, what Jack wrote made me think about her. (Ruefully picks at his hair.) I'm really distracted by our conversations.

THERAPIST:

How does Jack's writing make you think of your mother, though?

EVAN:

Talking about his mama, that's how my mama was for me.

THERAPIST:

(sighing) Yeah…

EVAN:

It also made me remember how protective Jack was over me. That Marco kid he mentioned, he was my older brother's age, but bigger than grown men. And what he didn't mention is that he eventually did punch him a little bit after that. That kid Marco was messing with my younger brother one day, and my older brother came to stop him, and Marco got in his face, so my older brother walked away. But then out of nowhere, Jack—who has always been short—jumped in Marco's face. And I don't remember what Marco said, but I remember he sort of laughed at this little boy challenging him, and then Jack punched him right in the mouth. I was never trying to encourage fights, but that was amazing. And Jack just stood there, not caring that Marco could kill him. Marco never really messed with Jack again.

THERAPIST:

It's clear he loved you, Evan.

EVAN:

Man, more and more I can see why he didn't want to talk to me because that's not how I treated him.

THERAPIST:

Well, keep writing to him, maybe you will both discover
why that is.

Evan sends another email.

To: Jackson (10)

I do remember my

younger brother

following you around.

I remember being

mad about it too.

By this time,

my older brother

and sister were

getting into trouble

worrying my mama
who'd been working
extra hours

to find the football money
I'd worked up the courage
to ask her for.

We didn't play
for the Falcons

as Jeffrey's mom
suggested.

They were too

expensive.

We played for
a Pop Warner team

called the North Side Tigers.

So that summer

me, Roger, and

my little brother

were standing in

line as our new

coaches passed out

jersey numbers.

As rookies,

we had to wait

for the veteran players
to take their pick.

I had my eye on

the number 80

for Jerry Rice.

So when coaches

held up the

jersey, instead

of reaching

out and pleading

like the other rookies,

I tried going still and silent,
in hopes of standing out.

And it worked.

Man, that was a moment.

I just knew then

I was destined

to be a pro athlete.

Then during

opening week,

I questioned

the whole

professional

athlete plan.

Headaches

from near dehydration,

aching muscles
I didn't know existed.

Sore neck from hitting drills
while supporting a heavy helmet,

and grown men screaming at us
to work harder

in 95-degree weather.

My natural talent was

apparent right off.

The veterans were cold

toward rookies

unless you had talent
and drive.

But I found

common ground
with fellow newcomers.

Roger got to show off

his brute strength
bringing the aggression

he used in creek fights

onto the field,

quickly becoming

a star on the team.

That year, I learned

being late to practice

would earn me extra

hill sprints. That missing

practice could cost

me my starting position.

I learned nothing
came easy and
how to keep going

when you just wanted
to lay down.

I didn't admire my coaches.
I admired football itself.

I had a dad, kind of,
but football became

my father.

Me, Roger, and

my younger brother

expressed our

undying love
for football

and the life

being an NFL player

could provide.

We played,

watched,

and spoke
about the game so much,
we became

almost as in sync
on the field,

as you and I were
on the court.

We created private signals

for future showdowns

against my older brother
and his friends.

We got serious fast.

A loss or a bad play

kept us up at night.

Though, I envied my younger brother,
still able to run to the river

to play tag or build forts
with other neighborhood kids.

From: Jackson (11)

I felt even more
left out when you three

got so into football.

        Then you started to be

        friendly with those

        preppy white kids,

        like Jeffrey Hall.

                It was kids

                like him that always

                reminded me that

                those adults slashing

                the air with their

                finger at my behavior

                were full of shit.

I was labeled

a bad kid.

Or maybe I was having

delusions of grandeur,
to believe I still had
that kind of effect on you.

Evans sends another email.

To: Jackson (12)

I don't want you

to feel I'm naïve.

I did get

friendly
with those

"preppy kids."

95

But I was never

close friends with them.

They gained me

access to places
I don't believe you
ever got to go.

I got to be around

their parents,

study how

they handled life with

more resources

than you and I

ever had.

I found navigating

that world

exhausting
as those folks
only responded

to a chipper version

of me. I could sense
their constant fear
that I'd become

the angry one

they were expecting.

Seeing us

rap, play sports, or riot
on TV is the closest

most of those kids

on the North Side

got to black people.

Seeing someone like you
at school

matched the expectations
they built from
what was shown on TV.

I don't mean

you did anything wrong,
but you walked around with

an unkempt afro, dashiki backpack,

and a smile like Seattle's sun,

there, but not often seen.

You were quiet,

suspicious of everyone,
and they all knew
you would fight.

Knowing the exhaustion

that came with being around

those kids, I had to

make a decision

our first day

of middle school.

My mama dropped me off.
I heard my name called:

It was Jeffrey Hall

and the "preppy kids."

I felt like you
in that moment.

I didn't want to be bothered

with fake laughs and smiles

nor did I want to explain myself.

So I shook my head

and walked on.

I wish I'd been able

to consistently hold

that conviction

throughout my life.

Or better yet,

that I stayed

closer to you.

Still, I'm glad

I did it then.

I was captivated

by the diversity of

the school.

North Side District

allowed busing
from the brand new

suburb on the East Side

while their schools
were under construction.

The East Side black
and Asian families

mixed with the Mexican

and white population

in the North made for
a colorful two years.

Dodging the

long stares

coming my way
from those noticing
I was a shorter, darker version
of my pecan-colored
older brother,
I went in search

of Roger,
and when I found him,
I found you, too.

Did we get closer

in middle school

because of
the American Dream Club

with Dr. Willis?

That first week,

she found me

in the quad
during lunch,
just as I'd seen her
track down all the other

black students

one by one.

"And what is your name, young man?"
She wore black reading glasses and short black hair,
permed straight.

"Uh, Evan."

"Hi, my name is Dr. Willis. I'm your assistant principal,"
she said, extending her hand.

"Have you signed up for the American Dream Club?"

I remember

shifting around,

trying to buy time.

I had read the flyers,

but really didn't know

much about it,

just that I was supposed to.

"No, uh, I am about to go do it," I lied.

"Good! We have a meeting in five minutes, in Room 11,
ok?!" she said, walking away.

"Ok," I said, practically standing at attention,
as the tin pan that held my pizza roasted my fingers.

That's when I met Ty.

"She scare you, too?"

"Nah," I lied again.

"Oh, she scared me. I heard black teachers go harder on
black students because we supposed to know better," he
said, shrugging.

As you know,

I had never had
a black teacher.

"She seems coo', though," Ty went on.

"You walking up to Room 11?" I asked. I remember his
short curly hair,

heavily plaqued teeth, ashy elbows, and the same black
jeans he wore each day.

"Yeah, I will walk up with you, but I need to see if
somebody
will let me borrow some money. I didn't eat lunch,"
he said, touching his stomach, looking everywhere but at
me.

"Ah man, sorry, I spent all mine," I said.

He finally looked at me as if he was surprised I was there.

"Oh, nah, I wasn't talking about you," he said, going back
to scanning the area.

"I wonder if Dre will let me borrow something," he
mumbled to himself.

"Want a piece of my pizza?" I asked.

His eyes quickly flashed to my hand.

"Oh, alright, but just give me some of the crust,
I'm not trying to take yo' whole lunch."

Had I known his scheme,
I would have let him starve that day
for this turned into an everyday thing.

I thought kids on

the East Side had
a little money, so
I figured if he was
asking somebody like me,
he must be worse off.

But one cold day,
I had enough
as I folded my small, circle
pizza to fit into my mouth,
crust and all,
and took my time
as it made its way
down my throat.

When I saw Ty bring in
his own bagged lunch,
something only kids
with money did,
I thought of all those
extra bites I'd given him
that my skinny behind
could have used
while he slunk off with my food
like Templeton
in Charlotte's Web.

I never expected much
out of our friendship
after that, which is probably
the case with most of my friendships.

The less I expect,
the less people can
disappoint me.

Still, Ty and I
were always together
because we shared classes.

Roger never found

his place in middle school,
though I know you
hung out with him
after school sometimes.
But he didn't fit with the preppy kids
and, though Dr. Willis
welcomed him
to the American Dream Club,
the other black kids
gave him an icy greeting,
and he never came back.

I do know he, too,
felt I left him behind that year.

Evan receives another email.

From: Jackson (13)

Roger did hang out with me.

But remember he broke his foot

in the beginning of y'all's third year

playing football?

> *His parents let him miss*
>
> *a lot of school that year, too.*

> *The American Dream Club*
>
> *was fun, but challenging.*

Ty was right,
Dr. Willis
was not playing
with us.

> *She immediately*
>
> *broke down*
>
> *the club plan*
> *to fundraise*
>
> *for an end-of-year trip*
> *to Great America.*

> *Which meant*
>
> *we had to sell*
>
> *those Caramel*
>
> *Apple Pops and*

chocolate bars

around campus.

We had to study
for the Jeopardy show

we put on for
our eighth grade classmates.

During lunch,

she had us

learning about

Medgar Evers

and other civil rights leaders

our history classes

didn't highlight.

Dr. Willis was on edge

weeks leading up

to our Jeopardy show.

She was the only

black administrator

on the North Side.

And she was not going to let us
succumb to stereotypes

in front of the school

on her watch.

INT. EVAN'S ROOM — DAY — MID-MARCH
2015

To: Jackson (unsent draft)

Erykah Torrey

asked me out

on the first day

of seventh grade

without ever

introducing herself.

As did

Molina Sanchez

after the first trimester

through a written letter.

I said no to both.

Me and you

used to

write about

our future

wives when

we were younger.

I figured

I would end

up marrying

Halle Berry

one day,

so there

was no need

to waste my time

on anyone

else.

You said

you would

marry Claire

Huxtable, which

then made me

realize that's

exactly who

I wanted to

marry too, so you

were nice

enough to share.

As we got

older and

interest in

girls became

a real thing,

as soon as I

was asked out
for the first time,
I realized I couldn't

put forth the effort

to be a
decent boyfriend.

Roger's dad

also used to

tell us to

stay focused

on our school

and sports, don't

worry about the

girls, which

I found to

be sound

advice.

But what if

I still wanted

the feeling

of being admired?

INT: EVAN'S ROOM — MID-DAY

Evan still on his bed, writing, the clock showing hours have passed.

To: Jackson (unsent draft)

I watched the crowd
during that Jeopardy show,
found myself
both embarrassed

and angry.

I eyed those

"preppy kids,"

noticed they never lost

interest because

they never had any.

It could have been
a middle school boy thing.

But I couldn't help

feeling offended.

We'd worked hard
to put the show together

and, since our topics weren't

about black entertainers,

they lost interest?

It just

INT: EVAN'S ROOM.

Evan is still at his laptop struggling to draft an email when he sees a notification that he has an incoming message from Jack.

From: Jackson (14)

Warm weather

and heightened

testosterone

made us all wilder
by the end of eighth grade.

> *You remember*
>
> *Dara, don't you?*
>
> *She had that*
>
> *auburn red hair*
>
> *and the*
>
> *biggest ones*
>
> *in school.*

>> *She was discussed*
>>
>> *by all of us boys*
>> *in the American Dream Club.*

And I'm sure at yo'

football practices,
like she was on the bus

on the seventh grade

basketball team.

She liked

the East Side boys.

Ty always told me
how she showed her breasts
to him and a few of the guys

behind the gym.

You said

you hadn't

seen them.

I hadn't either.

But that all

changed

the last week

of school.

"The code call is hooty hoo, y'all," Ty told us
when me, you, and the East Side boys circled up shirtless outside of
the pool.

. His lips had a light

chatter and

he wore beads

of water

on his curly head
as he'd already

taken a dip.

I was quiet,

but didn't want

to seem

intimidated.

You laughed

nervously along.

We all had

school-issued goggles in hand,

ready for the call.

"Aight, I will go talk to her, y'all get in," said Charles,
the tallest and most confident of us.

The pool was

packed with

eighth graders.

We slipped into

the shallow

end and spread out

to avoid obstructing

the others' view,

yet remained

close, like a small

pod of Orcas.

"Hooty hooo."

I took a deep

breath and

plugged my nose.

Dara submerged

and paddled

to remain below
the surface
in the deep end.

She scanned

the underworld

and immediately

spotted a few

kids not part of

the pod—

        who'd clearly

        got the drop

        on our plan

        and lingered

        with anticipation.

                Dara quickly

                aborted the mission.

We came

up for air,
knowing it best

to wait

until the intruders

lost interest.

        That took

        five minutes,

        and soon Ty,

who had

moved towards

Dara's end

of the pool,

shouted out,

"Hooty hooo."

This time, it was

just us.

Dara scanned

around once again
to confirm.

And then she

released them
from her bikini.

We had

two short

seconds

to admire

before Ty—

reached for

a voluptuous

left breast.

Immediately, she

smacked away his hand,
pulled on her top,

swam up for air.

We poured

out of the pool,

howling, and circled

up again.

"Ty, why did you do that?" Charles asked.

"I couldn't take it anymore."

I loved sharing

that time with you.

We had

the American Dream

Club together, but

that wasn't enough.

So I played basketball
in seventh grade
in hopes of recapturing

our chemistry

on the court.

Ty thought

I didn't go out for

the eighth grade team
because I didn't get much

taller, but that wasn't it.

      It was because

      it was no

      longer fun.

            You used to

            play with

            less care.

You didn't play

basketball the

next year either,

because you said

you wanted to

focus on football.

      ~

      The East Side was finishing

      their new high school

      by the end of summer.

I didn't want

to go back to being

one of the few

black kids.

So I asked Trese

her rent budget.

I was mindful

that any place

that required a

"credit score check"

was off limits.

I took daily

walks to 7-11

and scoured

the newspaper's

classifieds,

memorizing the

few possible

listings to recite

to her later.

I even biked

to the East Side

and stood outside

a few of the places—

> *hoping the house would*
>
> *magically give itself to me*
>
> *after acknowledging*
>
> *my dedication.*

INT: EVAN'S ROOM — NIGHT, THE SAME
EVENING.

Evan starts typing as soon as he's done reading.

To: Jackson (15)

News of me
not being able

to attend the new

East Side High School

came fast.

My mama

was then

head custodian

at a school
on the East Side,

so she made it clear
we couldn't afford
to live there.

I found

some peace

that eighth grade summer
by spending time

with Roger again.

He invited me
on a family camping trip

way up north
in Whiskey Town,

three hours away,
the furthest
I'd ever been from home.

When we arrived,
Roger's dad
helped set up

the tent
Roger and I
would share.

His parents

had a larger tent
twenty yards to our right,

which they shared
with his baby brother.

Roger's grandparents

slept in the camper

attached to their truck
with Roger's little sister.

The next day,

Roger's dad took

the two of us
on a late afternoon

lake cruise
in his grandpa's ski boat.

We sighted

bald eagles poised

to drive their talons
into a trout.

Small islands,

expensive boats,

even an old Gold Rush camp
underneath the lake.

"We will see who can hold on the longest when we go biscuiting tomorrow," Roger said.

"What's biscuiting?" I asked.

"You never been water skiing before?" Roger's dad asked. As he spoke, he waved his hands, which were hardened from long days of working a hammer.

His hair was long,

tied into a bun to show off

his double ear piercings.

He was a handsome man,

ruggedly gentle,

though easily irritated.

When he asked
a simple question,
the words still

came out hot.

I shook my head no,
surprised he'd ask,

as on the drive up
I said I'd never been
camping.

Roger loved

the man. They

laughed, spent
quality time,
but there was

no doubt

Roger's fistfights

in the creek

came as a release

for his pent-up anger

toward his dad.

After dinner,

there was

a session of

s'more making.

I remember

the silence,

the smell of

wild vegetation and

the burning wood

we used to melt

our marshmallows

to our liking.

I noticed

how peaceful

our surroundings were,
yet for so much

of my life,

camping was

everything
my mama

tried to avoid,
knowing one
missed paycheck

could land us all
in tents in the woods.

"Yo, Evan, grab those pack of Oreos," Roger whispered
as we cleaned up for the night.

"No, man, your parents said there's bears out here,"
I replied in the same heavy whisper.

"We'll finish 'em before the bears come out," Roger said
confidently.

Another snack

did sound good,

but so did my life.

I decided not to argue;
Roger was stubborn.

Plus, I already

recited his rebuttal

in my head.

"You never even been camping, I do this all the time."

So I just ignored him

and continued to clean.

"All right, we are done, I am going to bed. Goodnight,"
Roger suspiciously announced.

"Do you guys need help with anything else?" I asked.

They didn't.
So me and Roger
headed toward our tent.

In the wild,
pitch black

takes on

a new meaning.

Without the

moon reflecting

over the lake,

it felt like

the darkness

was thick.

I woke up

hours later

to slow, rhythmic pops.

"Roger, Roger," I whispered, shaking him awake.

"What, what?"

"Listen!" I said now, fully sitting up.
The singing crickets filled the silence.

"I don't hear…"

"Shhh…" I cut him off.

Pop…pop…pop

"Oh shit, you think it's a bear?"
Roger asked, now sitting up too.

"I don't know."
Roger fumbled around for the entrance zipper.

"Hey, no!" I whispered-shouted, tapping his back.

He slowly unzipped,

glanced out,
and turned to me to whisper.

"Evan, look!"

In the thick of darkness,
I saw

two sets of eyes
50 yards from our tent

heading in our direction.

Pop…pop…pop

I zipped the

tent tightly and

rounded on Roger.

"You bring those Oreos in here?"

"Oh, shit, I forgot to eat them."

"What?" I said in a voice as high as a whisper could go.

"Let's just be quiet, and hopefully they will leave," Roger suggested.

"Hungry ass bears?" I snapped.

But I knew

I didn't have
a better idea.

Setting his dad

or the bears

off was not ideal.

So we laid

back down

on our backs,

eyes opened

to the darkness—

listening as

whatever it

was, moved

closer.

Before we got

a chance to

break out

into a panic,

we heard:

"HEY, GET OUT OF HERE, GO ON!"
Roger's dad used a booming voice.

Roger quickly unzipped

our tent again

as we poked

our heads out

to see his dad

holding a flashlight

and two large black

bears scampering between

our two tents

and off into the woods.

Roger zipped

our tent, and

we returned to

lying on our backs.

Eyes still

wide open.

Hearts drumming

in our chests.

"You guys ok?" his mom called.

"Yeah!" we said simultaneously in our normal voices.

"Ok, goodnight, they won't come back," she assured us.

"Ok!" we replied.

I let all return

back to stillness

for a full eight

seconds before

I rounded

on Roger again,

talking through

my teeth, this time

while going

back to a heavy

whisper.

"You grab those fucking Oreo's and throw them

far from this tent."

He reached

into his

sleeping bag

and gently carried

out the plastic sliver

of Oreos as if

he was a

mama kangaroo
holding her

baby joey—

unzipped our

tent and launched

it out with

everything

he had.

That was

the age when

your body

started to betray you.

Like all new

teenagers, I

found myself

embarrassed by

the galaxy full of

small planets

my face became

some mornings.

Or when

I had to

sag my pants,

not for style

but because

they could

no longer

cover my

legs after

a sudden

three inch

growth spurt at

the end of

eighth grade.

But some things

didn't seem to register

as embarrassing.

I don't know why
that was.

I always had
a husky voice, so
it's possible that
the pride I had
in never having
my voice crack
while answering
a teacher's question
created a blind spot.

And left me naïve
of other changes
that came
at that time.

The next morning,

I walked out for

breakfast to

hear Roger

retelling parts

of last nights

event without

incriminating himself.

"Grandma, you know when we step on sticks and they
crack?

Well, they pop when bears do it."

"Good morning, Evan, want some breaaakfast?"
said his sweet old, white-haired grandmother.

"Good morning. Yes, please," I said,
starting to rub the night dust from my eyes,

I stopped when I felt Roger's glare on me.

After breakfast,

we went to

the lake to

biscuit.

I tried every

excuse to get

out of it without

directly saying

I was scared.

It didn't

help that Roger's

parents were

having fun with him by

not admitting

they were

driving the

boat slower

with me.

Feeding

his animal

like competitive

spirit.

For Roger

became adamant

that I do

it two more

times after I

unintentionally

showed him up

by not getting flipped

into the water

on my first

try.

Back at camp,

Roger and I

set off to find

the Oreo's

he threw the

night before.

It didn't

take long

as we came

across the

empty wrapper

split open without

a crumb remaining.

"Hey, why did you walk out to breakfast with a boner this morning, man? I think you scared my grandma," Roger finally confronted me.

"What?"

"Yeah, weren't you embarrassed?" Roger went on asking. "You could have at least tucked it in."

"Oh man, I promise, I didn't even know," I said.

"How could you not know?" he asked, starting to laugh. I never paid close attention up until that point of how ridiculous his laugh was. It could be infuriating in one moment and contagious in the next. For it had a bit

of a hoarse, chain smoker's quality to it, as his tongue rolled from

his mouth.

"I don't know. I walked out to breakfast a few months ago at home, and my dad and older brother started laughing saying I had a tent in my pants. Now I know what they were talking about," I admitted, shrugging my shoulders.

We laughed.

He told me

I need to

do something

with that.

We talked

about North

Side High.

Being in that

district and

the inevitability

of us both

having to

go to that

school.

We talked

about football.

How North Side

High hadn't been

any good in

years and

how we

planned to

change that.

We didn't

hang out

much at school

during our middle

school years,

yet in many

ways Roger was

still the kid

getting into

fights in the

creek.

He balanced

his occasional

street fight

with his refusal

to drink and party.

Like me,

his mission

was still to

play ball.

Some things

hadn't changed

while everything else

around us was.

From: Jackson (16)

Our steps were slow

and methodical.

> *Each time my shoe*
>
> *stepped on a tiny branch,*
>
> *it startled me,*
>
> *knowing there were wild pigs*
>
> *that ran men up trees*
>
> *in the area.*
>
> *"We got to be quiet; my dad will beat my ass*
> *if he catches us," George Mendoza whispered.*

I slowed my pace

even more, so he
could take the lead.

> *Also to give myself*
>
> *a head start*
>
> *in case we needed*
> *to break out*
>
> *into a sprint.*

It reminded

me of our times.

I really had no idea
what we were doing,

but the potential

danger excited me.

That summer

I, too, spent time

in the wilderness.

I'd never known
what George's pops did.

I just knew he had a ranch
somewhere on the East Side.

George spent

many Saturdays forced

to work there.

Wanting the company
of his peers, he'd ask his pops

if I could go along,

but his pops always said no.

Until that summer.

Sweat dripped

down George's brown face.

    Yet aside from the silk

    of a spider's web tangling

     in his black hair,
     his layers of gel
     kept it slicked back and neat.

         We arrived

        at an unfamiliar ranch,
         set up similarly

         to George's pop's
         around the corner,

          heavily shaded.

Parked inside

was an dusty, old, blue Chevy pickup
with a white camper shell
next to George's pop's

smaller, white Ford Ranger.

    Our whispers downgraded

    to emphatic, silent gestures.

        We reached a tree

        on the side of the property

        next to a wooden fence,

and climbed up.

Our little bodies covered
by its green and yellowish leaves

as we sat on the largest branch.

The light breeze

swayed the leaves,

giving us an open view
of the action.

Men standing next to
thoughtfully organized wire cages

that sat atop the reddish dirt
spoke softly in Spanish.

George and I tried

our best to listen in.
Being around the language
in the complex

let me understand some.

But these men

were speaking too fast
for me to keep up.

George's dad

stood tall and slender

holding a can of Pepsi

while his two comrades

held their prized fighters,

kneeling to attach sharp blades
onto their feet.

The roosters,

already irritated

by the sight

of each other,

were then picked up,

rocked back and forth,

just inches from touching

beak against beak.

"I love the green one,"
George whispered.

I smiled, accepting

the gentlemen's bet,

unaware this game
was played for keeps.

"I pick the red one."
I was captured by their colors,
vibrant as if painted on.

The fight lasted

no more

than a minute.

Brownish-black feathers
floated into the air.

The green rooster stumbled
as the red rooster

relentlessly flapped its wings,

driving its blades inside

the wounded animal.

"Is the green one dead?"

I asked, naïvely.

"Yeah, but the red one
is going to die too,"
George confirmed.

The green rooster

lay dead

as the red delivered more,
but less explosive, kicks,
before the winning man
broke it up.

Fresh blood

stained his hands as

he took off the blades.

The losing man

pulled a wad of cash
from his pocket,
flipped and counted it

before paying his debt.

"Let's go," George whispered
as we climbed down from the tree.

I knew better

than to ask questions

on our way back
to his pop's ranch.

Or to appear concerned.

Though I was.

But all I could do

was adapt,

which I did

after ripping

into the flesh of a pig
his pops caught

and butchered

a week prior.

~

155

On a rare day
when George

didn't have to work
at the ranch
or rub shoulders

in their small apartment
with his family (made crowded
by the arrival of an uncle
the year before),

        he had the place

        to himself.

                His family had gone

                to place a down payment

                on a house in rural Sacramento.

So we hung out

on his balcony
after searching
his uncle's pockets

for loose weed

we could smoke

from a soda can.

        Our neighbor Monica
        and her friend Ce Ce

        gave us the eyes

as they walked below

toward the river.

I felt Marcel's

influence immediately.

All he ever

was trying to do
at that point

was find an empty house

to take a girl.

And here we were
with a golden opportunity.

I never expected
anything would come of it.

I secretly hoped
they would be too shy

to hang out with us,
so I'd have an out

whenever I bragged
to Marcel about what
"almost happened."

We were still on the balcony

when they came up from the river.

I had seen Ce Ce

around before,

but now she was

developed and

experienced.

I was none of these,

so to compensate,

I met her with

that puffed-up

confidence. As soon as

they came upstairs,
I knew she was prepared

to call my bluff.

I matched her

by insisting

she should follow

me into George's room.

She did—

and her clothes slid

off her golden body
without my help.

She kissed

me and bit

my bottom lip.

Lifted my shirt.

Yanked at my shorts until

they fell to the floor,

my boxers still entangled.

She paused
only briefly

to rip the wrapper

with those same teeth.

She ordered me
to lay on my back,
as she climbed on

and guided me

inside her.

Her hip thrust
sank my little body

into the mattress,

as she tilted her chin
and arched her back—

allowing her

*long black hair
to lightly brush
her bottom.*

*Though my innocence
had already been seized
by my childhood,*

*She took what was left
as the soundtrack was
the bass of the bed*

hitting the wall,

*the crackling of latex
unwrapping, and her angelic vocals.*

*My sexual ineptness
was exposed as she shifted*

her hands from the bed

to my chest to provide

more leverage for her straddle.

*She was in charge
and reminded me*

each time

*by forcefully pulling
my hands to caress*

her dark brown nipples.

Her upper lip glistened.

The pressure

on my boney pelvis

was uncomfortable—

which my

face gave away,
for each time
I felt a need

to grimace,
her lips softly met mine.

I felt younger

than I was

that day.

And when we

finished, all

I wanted to

tell her was—

I lost my virginity

the same day

I had my first kiss.

INT. THERAPIST'S OFFICE — DAY — EARLY
APRIL 2015

THERAPIST:

...What did you feel about Jack losing his virginity that
summer?

EVAN:

It didn't surprise me.

THERAPIST:

Why not?

EVAN:

It's pretty normal growing up how we did. My mom had
my sister when she was 19. And something Jack didn't
mention, but you know our neighbor George Mendoza he
spoke of?

THERAPIST:

Yes...

EVAN:

Well, his family eventually did move out to Sacramento at
the end of that summer. But before that, we found out his
uncle that lived with him, who was in his forties, got my

sister pregnant when she was 18, and had already been physical with her a year before that.

THERAPIST:

Oh no, and your sister must have been vulnerable, not only being a kid, but having no male role model. And here comes this grown man being nice to her, I bet.

EVAN:

Yeah, exactly. Anyway, I have always seen young kids have babies because they came from broken homes and somehow think a child is going to fill up some of that emptiness, but it never works.

THERAPIST:

No, it never does.

EVAN:

But I did the same thing, tried to find things to fill that emptiness. I just didn't do it by having a kid early, which is what I plan to write to Jack about.

To: Jackson (17)

My older brother had taken over
my sister's room
when she moved out
with George's uncle.

My small room

seemed massive

with just me

and my younger

brother left in it.

My sister did eventually
move back in
with our new niece,

Jackie. They slept

on a single mattress
on our living room floor.

~

I never realized

I was short

until Roger's grandfather

noticed I grew a few inches

and said,

"Evan, you got taller!
And all this time
I thought you would turn out
to be a runt."

The hundred

push ups

I started

to do before

bed each night

that eighth grade summer

sculpted a

body that

was not impressive

under a shirt. But

got attention once

ninth grade

PE rolled

around.

My older

brother had

been kicked

out of school

for selling weed

and was now

at a continuation

school.

It would have

been nice

to have a

junior in

high school

show me

the ropes.

Yet, instead,

his friends

assumed the role.

Most of

them were East Side

kids who had

to attend North Side

High and decided

to finish off

where they

started.

You and I

were the

only black

boys in our class.

The majority of us

black folks were

upperclassmen.

I never knew

if my brother

asked them to

look after me,

but right away

they literally

pulled me

over to their

post—

on the brick steps,

that led to the

front side

of Channing

Hall. A

high traffic

area that

faced the

quad.

They were

on top of

the food chain

in all aspects.

Every beautiful

upper class girl

us freshman

guys dreamed about,

spent time

near their post.

The girls would

play flirt with me,

which I half

loved, half

hated.

Popularity is

a strange thing.

Who doesn't

want to be

appreciated?

I know I

do, but on some

level, I understood

you could never

really trust it.

So, I only

lasted a

few days

at their post

and found

Roger with

the kids our age.

Like the North Side

of town, the high

school was mostly

segregated.

Outside of a

few exceptions,

Mexican and

white students

stayed with

their "own."

Remember the
fights between some
of them?

For me,
that was
confusing.

Because I
knew most
of the Mexican
kids, but
few of them
played football,
some were
placed into
ESL classes,
some started
gang banging.

While at

that point,

I was actually

starting to

hang out

with some

of the white

kids on the

team besides

Roger.

To do that,

I had to

tap into the

skills I

developed

during my

brief interactions

with those

"preppy kids"

at the

end of our

time in elementary

school.

And as you

learned to

understand Spanish

being around

the complex,

I learned to

exchange

"y'all"

for

"you guys"

and

"finna"

for

"going to,"

to make

communicating

easier.

In some cases

that worked.

Backfired in others.

As it comforted

some white kids.

Yet the others

who listened

to hip hop,

but had

never been

around a large

number of

black people,

figured they knew

how we

were supposed

to act and talk.

Which convinced

them that

I wasn't

"really black."

Writing this

now, makes

me understand

why you were

even more

quiet and to

yourself.

I knew from watching
my big brother

get pigeonholed
by misperceptions,

that if I was going

to survive

those four years,

I would need

to learn to

pick my battles.

So once again,

I started to

smile more

than I wanted to.

Remain more

calm than

anyone should—

as the casual

racist

comments

came at me.

I saved my

blow ups

for the overt

ones.

The kind that

even our principal

would have

an issue with—

in case I

was sent

to his office

after I took

to violence.

I became a master at

compartmentalizing

friendships, treated some

as if they were close,

when in actuality

my only real friend

was Roger.

By the time

my younger brother

got settled into

North Side High

my sophomore year—

my carefree disposition

was here to stay.

I noticed how he looked at me

as if I was no longer recognizable.

Yet with all

my good intentions,
and "good" behavior,

I was never able
to translate that
into the classroom.

My coaches sat me down
to explain I had the talent
for a scholarship, but

recruiters would run
if I continued down

that same road.

From: Jackson (18)

I didn't get to spend

a lot of time with you,

but I did know

about yo' struggles
in school.

People expected

little from me, but

you were on a pedestal.
They all saw you as smart,

but helped you anyway.

Girls would let you

copy in math.

Yo' teammates

would jot down
the answers
during their biology tests

so you would be eligible

for the coming football season.

You charmed

yo' way

into the hearts of

the North Side.

You appeared

spoiled and arrogant.

Like you just knew
yo' talents could outduel
yo' poor classroom efforts.

As for me, I

never believed

school was a

good measurement

for my natural abilities.

So I gave little effort.

I did well

in my art classes.

That's where

I met Tina.

The girl who got me
to stop smoking and drinking
at least for a little bit.

Of course you

remember her, right?

Though given how beautiful
she was and how she was one of the few

black girls in school, and

from a large family,

she wasn't talked about much.

You think it's because

the friends she had

were labeled

"Jesus freaks?"

Or because she was

short and quiet?

It's likely because

her parents were strict
and Christian.

The kind that never

missed Sunday service, youth group,

or Bible studies.

I was surprised

she liked me.

She used to always

tease me, telling me
to smile more.

She wasn't allowed

to date until she was 16

nor hang out with me

alone.

Which allowed me

to reap all the benefits

of sexual repression.

As we ditched class
and did it in her friend's

living room.

On hikes in

the North Side hills.

On bus rides

to school dances.

In the back seat

of her parents'

minivan.

I had come a long way
from my time with Ce Ce.

I was causing trouble

by secretly defying her parents—

but I was

no longer

defying the law.

I started to go to church

every Sunday

in the South Side

with Trese

and my aunties—

which led Tina's parents

to believe I was
a nice, Christian boy

and to give Tina
a little more freedom.

I felt strange being treated
with a respect at church
I was unaccustomed

to receiving elsewhere.

And as always,

I did wonder

if you saw

the change in me.

To: Jackson (19)

I did notice

a change in you
during that time,

and though I didn't

go to church,

you know

my mama did.

I always have respect

for anything positive
someone uses
to keep their life in order.

You are right about

my efforts in school.

It definitely was

connected to

my struggles at

home.

This was around

the time

Roger's family

bought a new house
in the up-and-coming

East Side,
yet he was able to stay
at North Side High.

From: Jackson (20)

Yes, it was.

It is also the time

we lost contact
for good.

> *I heard y'all*
>
> *were moving to the South Side.*
>
> *I was surprised*
> *you were actually*
>
> *excited.*

> > *I wondered if*
> >
> > *you had forgotten*
> >
> > *it was crazier than*
> >
> > *the complex.*

Then I learned

while it was technically

the South Side,

it bordered

the East and shared
more with that neighborhood.

> *Yo' sister followed*

yo' mama's footsteps,
was working as

a night custodian

at North Side High.

Since they liked her
and you and yo'

younger brother

were star football players,
they let you remain in

the North Side school district too.

Yo' mama finally had

enough, which meant

yo' pops wouldn't

be coming with you.

He still had

family in New York

that offered

him a place

to stay.

The day he left,

yo' mama was at work;

yo' sister was dropping you off late
at school, before taking yo' pops
to the train station.

I was late

as usual, so

caught a ride with you.

Third period had started.
You asked yo' sister

to drop us on the backside of school,

so we could slip in unnoticed.

I will never forget
the weather outside,

because it matched the mood
inside her '96 Sebring—

cold and gray.

I was curious

how you were going to handle

yo' goodbye with yo' pops;
I had never really

hugged a man.

I sat directly behind yo' sister

in the back seat, watching
yo' pops in the passenger seat.

He looked healthy,

which I assumed was because
he'd been hoping

yo' mama had a change of heart.

Then I watched you.

Trying to manage

yo' unease by playing

with yo' niece

who sat next to you

in her car seat,

a beautiful gift
yo' family had received
from George's uncle's crime

Jackie.

We pulled

into the back lot.
Yo' sister stopped.

No one got out of the car.

No one knew what

to do. Until finally

yo' pops spoke.

"Ok, Evan, love you," he said, still facing forward.

"Ok, love you too, man!" you replied before rushing out.

Students

were in class.

The campus was silent.

As were we,

outside of

our synced steps.

It was a sad day for you,
regardless of yo' lack
of relationship with yo' pops,

but I hadn't felt
this close to you
since we were kids.

I wanted you
to write out
how you felt,

share it with only

me.

I was angry with you,

but I was dying

for us to write again.

We had a lot
of catching up to do.

I could feel

you on the verge

of breaking down.

You were ready
to say something.

I had no desire
to go to math.

I was ready
to leave school
all together.

I could tell

you were with me.

We passed

our entrance

for class,

passed through

the side parking lot.

Our bad grades
didn't matter any longer.

Nothing did.

We reached
the opposite edge,
near the back side

191

of Channing Hall.

I saw you

turn yo' head.

I did too

and noticed

Coach Fort,
with his blond spiked hair
and youthful good looks,

staring at you.

I don't know

if he saw me.

I didn't care

if he did.

I ran off.

When I glanced back,
I saw you turn right,

walk up the brick steps
of Channing Hall,

and go in to class.

THERAPIST'S OFFICE — DAY — MID-APRIL 2015

THERAPIST:

That was heart-wrenching to read, Evan.

EVAN:

Up until that point, that was the hardest year of my life.

THERAPIST:

Talk to me more about that.

EVAN:

First off, Jack was spot on with his memory of that day with my dad. But months before that day, I had dated this girl named Christy and, for the entire sixth months, I never invited her over to the complex.

THERAPIST:

Because you were embarrassed?

EVAN:

Definitely. She lived in one of the wealthiest neighborhoods on the North Side called Hawkings.

I used to have her drop me off down the street, but eventually she found out where I lived and showed up one night. Me and my younger brother were watching Jackie for my sister while she was at work, but then my dad showed up high.

THERAPIST:

Oh no.

EVAN:

Yes, I broke out in a full sweat and basically rushed her out.

THERAPIST:

(Sighs and shakes head sympathetically.)

EVAN:

There were fights every single day between my parents about his drug addiction.

THERAPIST:

Evan, I am really sorry.

EVAN:

(Squirms uncomfortably in his seat, looks out window.)

THERAPIST:

Yeah… sit with that.

EVAN:

In comparison, this may sound silly, but it made it worse that we had a horrible year in football.

THERAPIST:

Not silly, I can see how that could add to an already tumultuous time. And it sounds like you and this girl broke up around this time too.

EVAN:

Yeah, that wasn't so bad. I really didn't want a girlfriend at the time. She rightly broke up with me. I used to be kind of flaky with girls, as you could probably deduce.

THERAPIST:

I see… Tell me more about that time when Jack was walking with you. Did you feel close to him again?

EVAN:

I did, and he was right. I had been ready to walk off into the world and leave school and never go back. I don't know where we were going or how we were going to live our lives, but I was done with whatever I had been doing before. Then when I saw my coach, I took it as a sign.

Like he appeared out of nowhere for a reason, which was to keep me on the path I had been creating for myself.

THERAPIST:

Did you think Jack had your best interests in mind?

EVAN:

…I don't think he did. Jack had broken up with his girlfriend Tina, which was not a big deal because her parents were too strict for a guy like him. But he then went back to his old ways during that time.

THERAPIST:

Getting into fights?

EVAN:

Yeah, and walking around campus not saying a word to anyone.

THERAPIST:

And you didn't want to be around that.

EVAN:

No, I didn't. I feel bad, but I didn't.

THERAPIST:

I understand. And then your family moved to the South Side part of town?

EVAN:

Yep.

THERAPIST:

How was that for you?

EVAN:

It was nice to be around more black people. And it got wild around the corner, but our street was mostly quiet. And really, I just hung out with Roger on the East Side and some friends on the North.

THERAPIST:

And Michele?

EVAN:

And Michele.

THERAPIST:

Now remind me, who was it that met her first, you or Jack?

EVAN:

Jack.

THERAPIST:

Do you plan on bringing her up to him?

EVAN:

. . .

THERAPIST:

. . .

EVAN:

I don't think I have a choice.

INT. EVAN'S APARTMENT — EVENING.

Evan is typing at a desk in his apartment. Camera zooms in on his back and down to his fingers and the screen, where we see:

To: Jackson (21)

I have been reluctant
to talk about Michele.

Mostly because

I feel shame for

how I handled
what happened.
But I guess the only way

to do it is to dive in.

I know you

noticed her first.

I was there
for the whole

interaction.

There was something
about her.

Her lips were

full. Legs were

long.

Her face wasn't

done-up pretty,

but stripped-down

beautiful.

Yet I remembered

my dad's words:

"Never marry a white woman."

I was a little boy

when he said that

as I sat next to him
watching the O.J. Simpson trial.

I dated another white girl,
Christy, but I never

thought of marrying her.

With Michele,
even if I didn't think marriage,

I did think future.

She was from

Hawkings as well,
the neighborhood that felt

like a separate town

with a bowling alley,

golf course,

and grocery store.

I was supposed to be with

a Clair Huxtable.

It was my responsibility

to raise a family
with my black wife,

the two of us
beginning a legacy

of black excellence.

I wondered how
I'd share that life

with a blonde-haired,

blue-eyed girl.

How could

I pour salt

on the wounds

of black women

as I walked with her

hand in hand?

From: Jackson (22)

There are serious

challenges couples

have to address

when dating outside

of their culture.

    But that's one way

    we are different.

        I don't feel the

        need to explain

          myself.

If someone

has an issue with

someone I love,

I'll ask them

to let me know

when they get over

it.

    But let me

    get to the

    real issue—

        which is you not

        wanting me to

        know Michele.

You, like everyone else,
thought I wasn't
good enough.

I didn't just see
Michele that day,
I felt her.

She felt

me too.

Not merely

with the searing lust
of the planet Mars.

But also with the beauty

of the tender pluck
of a harp string.

I had Physical Science
with Michele
first period.

I never sat by her
because I was always late.

Which meant

we could never

partner up

during lab.

I do agree

with you

on her appearance.

She wore a face of beauty

with no expectations

of being admired.

Maybe because she wasn't
very popular, she wasn't

spoiled by the admiration

of teenage boys.

I was not

popular either

nor all that vocal.

Then here you came,
joining the track team

when she did.

Flirting with her as if

you were a carefree kid
from her neighborhood.

When I went to church,

Pastor Walker sermonized

on hate and the destruction

it caused the one hating.

To: Jackson (23)

I agree with you
about challenges

couples from different

cultures have to address.

I just wish I had acted

on it early on.

We went from

school night phone calls

to Michele meeting me
in the parking lot

after my games
senior year.

We weren't a couple.
As I'd done in past

relationships, I kept her
at a comfortable distance.

Then I got an early lesson

on how Michele
was unlike other girls.

After a game,

we planned to meet up

at a friend's house.

Instead, me and Roger

hung out late

with guys on the team,

getting into ridiculous things
like encouraging our running back
to streak outside Applebee's.

I didn't feel like
telling the guys

I was leaving

to see my non-girlfriend.

I just hoped

our night would end

early enough for me
to make a late appearance
to see Michele.

But that never happened.

No cellphones back then.

So I had to wait
to get home
on the South Side

to call Michele.

"Hey, I'm sorry about tonight."

"Who do you think you are?" she asked.
She cut me off every time I tried to apologize.

"I know you used to do this shit to other girls,
but don't ever think you can get away with that with me."

I had lost her trust
before I fully earned it.

When I finally asked her
to be my girlfriend

not long after,

she turned me down.

From: Jackson (24)

That story about

Michele telling you off
sounds like her.

I find the ones I trust most

always let us know

when we cross
their invisible lines.

I admire

that strength.
I grew up admiring it

in Trese.

Though you attempted
to keep her from me,

Michele and I still

spoke at times.

She called to let me know

she didn't get into Cal Poly.

> *Said she was playing*
>
> *with the idea*
>
> *of going with*
>
> *friends to*
>
> *Long Beach State—*

> > *but admitted*
> >
> > *that was only because*
> >
> > *she was too afraid*
> >
> > *to branch out on her own—*

she eventually settled on

Chico State,

a couple of

hours north.

> *I found out*
>
> *she loved*
>
> *to read.*

> > *I never got a chance*

but I believe
she sensed
the poet in me.

I thought of what it would be like

to write to her.

I thought

she would have liked it,

even if it wasn't her taste.

I had no

college plans.

Not even junior college.

Trese told me

I needed
to find a job.

Yo' older brother

offered to let me
trim his plants
for a few dollars

back when it was still illegal.

I surprised myself
by turning it down,

even if the money would have been nice.

Your brother told me
that silver and black '72 Mustang

you used to drive across town
came from his weed money—

and the DUI that left him

unable to drive it.

To: Jackson (25)

That's true about the Mustang.

Cost my brother lots of money,
but saved my mama
money and time
no longer having to cart me

and my younger brother

all around.

I'd kept on getting mediocre grades,
causing university coaches
to hang up after they heard.

But Butte Community College
was high on my and Roger's list
after one of our young coaches suggested it.

He set up a visit
for us to see the campus.

We didn't know much
about community college football,
but we soon learned a few schools

were perennial powerhouses.

Butte was

one of them.

To get there, we drove through

walnut orchards and sparse countryside,

then past large hills with flat tops
we would later find out

gave the college its name.

The school

was built into

a wildlife refuge,

spread out and extra green

that time of year.

We learned student-athletes

lived in the city of Chico,

a 20-minute drive from campus.
The coaching staff
would set us up with housing

if we decided to commit.

Roger committed.

It took until the end

of the summer

for me to commit

to live with Roger in Chico

and attend Butte College.

Financial aid

and my mama's help
allowed me to manage

the cheap rent

with no job.

First time I had

my own room

with our furnished apartment

enclosed by lavish gates.

Living in the

same town

as Michele

was never the

plan.

Yet since

it worked out

that way,

I shortened

the distance

between us

by inviting her over.

Our freedom and familiarity
drew us in.

The unexplored

brought us closer.

Which meant…

Well no,

not that.

That

took time.

She wouldn't even let me

kiss her at that point.

Mainly, we cuddled

while she fell asleep,
leaving me battling

numb arms and

relentless erections.

We weren't officially a couple,

but while she slept,

I still thought

of our future family

and football.

It all started to feel

possible.

So what I did next

still remains

a mystery to me.

~

Chico's blazing summers

in football pads

felt criminal.

Walking up

the concrete steps

to our apartment

after practice
felt like a full-time job.

'Til one morning

I walked into

the locker room,

grabbed my cleats,
left my playbook,

and drove the 20 miles

back home.

Roger was confused.

I hadn't mentioned

quitting before,

hadn't even thought of it.

From: Jackson (26)

Marcel was shot in the head
and left in the street.

His brother

happened to be
riding his bike

from his lady's house

when he found him

bleeding out.

I drove to

the hospital

with Trese.

None of

us expected

him to make it.

Somehow, he

came out

with just a scar

and remorse.

I feared my time
of pulling out a revolver

on the kids at the courts

219

had come back

to haunt me.

But he knew

the guy

who shot him
and was never going

to tell the authorities.

I knew Trese
wouldn't kick me out

after this.

She feared

what I would become
if she did.

I mostly stayed in

after that.

Not for fear of my life,

but to settle

Trese down.

From: Jackson (27)

I spoke to

Roger around

that time.

We had

one of those

relationships

that picked up

where we last sat it down—

as if nothing

had changed.

He had a girlfriend

who went to Chico State.

She then moved in
to a four-bedroom apartment

with him, his teammate "Good",
and another roommate.

I heard you were being

recruited by some big

colleges.

Then I

heard you were

on yo' way

back to Butte

that spring after

their fourth

roommate wanted

to break her lease.

I was happy

to hear yo'

younger brother

would not be

following you around.

It was clear you

hadn't figured

out where you

wanted to be.

Roger didn't directly ask

how I was doing,

but his call

was enough.

I hadn't heard

from Michele at

that time either.

It did hurt to

know you would

be close to her

again when I wasn't.

I started

leaving the

house more—

because Trese's

youngest brother

Uncle Stevie

came to stay

with us.

He, like all

of my aunties and

uncles, struggled

with drugs.

I always saw

him clean.

His words

always softly

spoken.

He got me

out the house

by taking me to a monthly

sit-down breakfast.

Which is something

I'd rarely done.

I remember

the first time

feeling guilty

for leaving our

dirty plates

on the table

when we left.

He woke me

up to help him

fix Trese's car.

We checked

the timing belt,

replaced the

air filters,

windshield

wiping blades,

and spark plugs.

And the man

could cook.

At one time,

a butcher.

Inheriting the

ancestral gift

of turning

low-quality food

into something

enviable.

I saw our time

spent together

coming to an end

before it happened.

I was on

the South Side

visiting my

grandmomma

and caught him

buying dope

in front of

an abandoned

Wal-Mart.

I didn't

say anything

to Trese, though

I wish I had.

Because within a few weeks,

he stole Trese's keys.

Police found the car

we'd worked on

abandoned, burnt.

A drug deal

gone bad.

After kicking him out,

Trese was blamed

by the family.

But that's

the way it

goes.

To: Jackson (28)

Michele abruptly

rolled off me,

onto her side.

The lights

that illuminated

the paths

of her condo

slipped through

her blinds.

I could see

her eyelashes

flicker.

She was

deep in thought.

It was 5 a.m.

Sleep deprivation

didn't help me understand

why our sultry moment

came to a halt.

"What are we doing?" she said softly, finally breaking her
silence.

"I mean, do I have to explain—?" I said.

"No, I mean with everything," she continued, cutting me
off.

I paused.

Allowed her

ceiling fan

to fill the awkward pause
while I tried
to crack this code.

I hadn't

asked her to

be my girlfriend

after being denied

in high school.

I'd thought it was clear
she wanted to

keep it casual.

Midday hangouts

were never our thing,

just the after-hours text or call.

I couldn't believe
she felt any pressure.

I then wondered

if I had missed

her subtle signals

for me to ask again.

"What are you talking about?" I asked.

"We can't do this anymore."

"What's going on?" I said sitting up.

"I don't think I trust you;
sometimes you're available,
then out of nowhere you're gone,"
Michele confessed.

I got it then.

That's right,
I was back
at Butte College.
Living in Chico
with Roger,
his girlfriend, and
his teammate Good.

I left for another
college, drew some

attention from recruiters

as a starter,

struggled to get along with

my coach and was

out after two semesters.

Roger called during

Christmas break,

suggested

I make a return.

Said there would

be an open room soon.

He spoke

with the coaches,

who admitted

they loved

my talent

enough to have

me back.

I moved back

to my mama's

on the South Side

during the holiday break

to wait for my room

to open up

in Chico.

I trained, adding

another ten

pounds of muscle.

I didn't tell

Michele

or even speak

to her.

I told myself

if I was going

to do it,

I needed

no distractions.

Roger's call

reminded me

of my goal.

Football must

come first.

I did slip up

once when

I returned to Chico.

It was that night

in Michele's bedroom.

It took a moment

to remind myself

of my main objective.

When my head

was clear,

I had my response.

"If you don't want anything to do with me, just let me know

so we don't have to continue to waste each other's time," I
said.

Her blinks

came slower.

She faced away from me,

looking in the opposite direction,
guarding herself.

Pulling her duvet

over her bare chest

as if I suddenly

became a stranger.

"I…don't want anything to do with you."

I slipped out of her place

within a minute.

From: Jackson (29)

I started to text
back and forth

with Michele

that spring.

We talked

about you.

I told her what I felt.

I told her

she wasn't

always getting

the real you.

When she asked
who the real you was,
I had to admit

I no longer knew.

I did say

the guy

you had become

would step over

anything or anyone

to get where he

needed to go.

I told her I was

surprised you hadn't

moved back home

for good.

Most popular high school

kids eventually do.

She even called

once, before leaving

on a spring break

trip with friends.

I couldn't relate.

She was out there

living her life; I wasn't.

Either way,

it was nice

she called.

To: Jackson (30)

The trainers spoke

with optimism

while their eyes

showed concern.

Said I might have

a high-ankle sprain.

Roger helped

me to the car.

It didn't happen

from being tackled

or an illegal play.

It was

in warmups

after catching

a five-yard pass

the first week

of spring practice.

My left foot

slipped. My right

foot caught

under my body,

all my

weight landed

on it.

I took my

shoe and

sock off to

see that my foot

had gone

purple at the

toes and

fat at

the ankle.

At home,

my new

roommate Good

helped me to his car

for a hospital visit

after seeing

my injury.

The doctor

circled the

area on my

ankle, confirming

a broken

tibia, which

would require

surgery, screws,

a metal rod.

Good's bald head,

nose piercing,

arm tattoos,

tree trunks

for legs were

deceiving.

Off the field,

he was gentle.

His family, too,

had little.

Still, he always

returned home

with plates of

food for us that his dad or

sister cooked

after visiting

his hometown

an hour away.

He called Michele

to update

her on my injury

that day.

She came

by that night.

When she entered

my room, I was

reminded she

was the

type of girl

I wanted

to marry one

day.

I asked

myself why

would I go

searching, when

the real thing

was right there?

I decided,

if it doesn't

work out between

us, it wouldn't

be from

my lack of

effort.

I started

to call her

to "check in"

on her during

the week—

looking past

any fear of

overdoing it,

just calling

because I

wanted to.

I invited her

over to

watch reruns

with me.

As she fell

asleep on me

as she had

before.

In a short time,

we were spending

several nights

a week

together.

I still refrained

from asking

her to

be my girlfriend.

I knew space was

needed to let trust

come organically.

From: Jackson (31)

I was

curious about

what you had

going on

during that time.

I will admit to

have rejoiced

when finding out

you were down

on yo' luck again.

Trese would

never appreciate

that kind of

twisted talk.

But it's true.

To : Jackson (32)

That is not

an easy thing

to read and still

I understand.

I decided

to apply to Sacramento

State, walk on

to the football

team, and earn

a scholarship that summer.

I applied,

I got in.

Meanwhile,

I remained

on the Butte football

team. Unable to

play on Saturdays due to

injuring my left

foot just as my right

one healed.

I stayed home

when the team

traveled for

games.

On one of

those Saturday's

is when I met

Tony.

He seemed

older than my

age of twenty-one.

Squat with

a manicured goatee,

broad shoulders,

baritone voice.

His light brown

skin glimmered

with sweat as

he approached

me at the apartments'

mailboxes.

"Excuse me, you know where the swimming pool area is?"
he asked.

"Yeah, just follow this path on the left. It's just around the
corner," I said.

"Ok, thank you. You play football?"

I told him.

He did too.

Mentioning that he was

from Washington

State.

Meeting up

with his high

school friend,

a fellow injured player

on my team,

to discuss

trying out

the following

spring.

After the brief chat,

he made it

back every day

to extend

our conversation.

From: Jackson (33)

Michele left

to study aboard

in Italy in

the spring.

I didn't hear

from her much

during those

six months.

Just one

phone call

attempt.

It was

choppy.

She couldn't

hear me, but

I heard her.

She wanted

to wish me

a happy birthday.

To: Jackson (34)

Michele's mom

gave me

and a couple

of her friends

calling cards
for Christmas
to save us from
massive charges.
With the time
difference,
we mostly
communicated
through email.

One of
the few times
we spoke
on the phone,
I said I love
you before hanging
up.

It just slipped
out.

The fear

of not hearing

her say it back

shifted me

into retrograde.

A revisit to

past behavior.

It was proven

in our next email.

She asked if

I said what

she thought

I said.

I denied it.

She took

two weeks

to reply.

When she

did, she wanted

to make it clear

that we were to

forever remain

friends.

I replied

with no reply.

I told myself

I gave it

true shot.

It was

time to move on.

By summer,

Roger decided

to hang up

the cleats.

His relationship

with his girlfriend

ended.

He was accepted

into UC Davis.

He now just wanted to

focus on school.

With his new college

only being a

20 minutes' drive

from Sacramento State,

we were

to remain roommates.

Eventually recruiting

my new friend Tony

as our third when

I learned he

decided to end

his playing days as well.

Michele returned

back to the States

early summer.
I got a call
after leaving
practice.

I tried
my best to
remain cold.

Since
getting to Sacramento,
I had a couple
of dates,
nothing serious.

It was more
about having a
fresh start.

I couldn't hold
the coolness

for long.

I know

love is difficult

to explain, but

maybe you

are right. You

are not the

first one to

suggest that maybe

I explain too

much.

Anyway, by

the end of

the call

at last, she

was my girlfriend.

Evan immediately begins to draft up another email to send.

To: Jackson (35)

I impressed

a few coaches

at Sacramento State

that summer.

I needed another

math class

which meant I

was scheduled

to be on the spring

roster.

Then the entire

staff was fired.

I never attempted

to convince Roger

to continue playing

after he gave it up.

After all of

our passionate

talks as kids,

I didn't have

much to say

about it.

My younger

brother, who was

on scholarship

at the University

of Arizona,

encouraged me

to reach out

to the new

coach.

I walked into

his office that

spring with

no appointment.

For a busy

Division I

coach, he

gave me his

full attention.

Even encouraging

me to come

back out.

I noticed

when I spoke

I was confusing him.

When I begin to

pay closer

attention to

my words it

sounded as if I were

inquiring, instead

of asking for

permission.

I left with

the when,

where, how

to show up

for practice.

Without providing

a definitive answer

if I planned

to show up.

Walking out

of the office

that day, I knew

why I hadn't tried

to convince Roger

to return to playing.

I too was done.

Too afraid to

let go.

Football was all

I thought I had.

I was secretly hoping

the coach

would say

"Sorry, we have our preferred walk-ons in mind already,
so there is not enough room for you on our spring roster."

Then I could

begin crafting

a story to

explain to that

future mystery

person that

asked me

what went wrong.

I felt unstable

on my walk

from the office.

Like I was

walking off

the edge of

Earth, into

the mouth of

the abyss.

I needed to skip
my history class
to gather myself.

INT. THERAPIST'S OFFICE — DAY — LATE MAY 2015

THERAPIST:

Talk to me more about what you most recently sent to Jack.

EVAN:

Ok, well a lot was going on. Not just being done with football. My dad got remarried and moved back to California.

THERAPIST:

Hear from him much when he was in New York?

EVAN:

Not at first, but when he got married, his wife would call and then hand him the phone.

THERAPIST:

How did that feel?

EVAN:

All right. I saw the effort. I was still insecure about my childhood. I didn't speak much about it. Not even to Michele. Without football, I—

Didn't feel as if you were enough?

EVAN:

Yes, I questioned why Michele would even want me. I didn't grow up like her. I wasn't one of those kids from Hawkings with money. So even though I knew I was done, I couldn't fully let go. It's like I needed permission.

THERAPIST:

From your mother?

EVAN:

Yep, she was an empty nester at that time. My two older siblings were in town, but had significant others, two kids a piece and their own places. So, I knew I had privacy, that's why I skipped class to go see her.

To: Jackson (36)

My timing

was perfect.

Knowing

my hour plus

drive from school

would get me to her
just after
she got home
from work.

I didn't call.

I was lost

in thought

on the way.

Nor have I ever
needed a reason
to return home

unannounced.

I let myself in,
noticed she wasn't

on the couch.

Saw a bag of

defrosting chicken

in the kitchen sink.

Heard gospel music

playing upstairs

and knew

she was enjoying

her bath.

She came

down a half

hour later.

I sat on her red-and-green
loveseat while she
sat on her couch.

We spoke for

some time 'til

it was time

to talk football.

"Ev, I don't want you to take this the wrong way,
I've always thought you had a lot of talent,

but I think you should just try something else;
you don't seem happy anymore."

"…Yeah," I said through a long sigh.

"When I sat you down all those years ago to watch those
movies,
football was never the plan. I just wanted you to see you
can do more
than what you see around you. And that you could go out
into the world
and see things no one in our family has been able to see."

"I know."

"I barely had the money to get y'all into football, but when
yo' older brother and sister started to get into a little
trouble, I figured whatever I was doing wasn't working. So
if I had to lose sleep and not eat to come up with the
money, then that's what I had to do."

I nodded.

"So put that same energy you had for football into
something else,

and you will be fine. Don't feel like you got to do this
anymore."

"How long have you noticed I wasn't happy with football?

And why didn't you say something?" I asked.

"Boy, I'm not about to tell you what to do. What if I was
wrong?
Shoot, I was recruited by a track coach when I was
younger,
but my mama wouldn't let me run, and one of the girls I
used to beat,
ended up going to the Olympic trials."

I nodded again

already knowing the story,
as she'd made sure

we remembered

where we got

our talent.

"My mama was just mean sometimes, though.
Everything changed after my daddy died
because then she married that man."

I knew "that man" was

her stepdaddy.

"It was like living in hell,
and I got caught up with drugs and alcohol,
had yo' sister and then you three boys,
but I didn't get myself together
until my mama kicked me out."

"Why did she kick you out?"

"Because I threatened to kill that man," she said matter-of-factly.

"What happened?"

"Y'all was still young, and I was still running the streets.
One night I asked him for a few dollars to buy some beer,
and he said he would give me money if I gave him some."

"What?

"Yep."

Our blinds were open.

The sky was now gray-blue.

Her moisturized brown

legs shone.

Her hair, wrapped

in black cloth,

seemed to frame

her slim face.

"I walked away from him, didn't say nothing, but another
day,
I found out he had asked the same from yo' auntie who
wasn't even 17,"
she said now, pulling up her long legs,
wrapping her arms around them for comfort.

"Oh no."

"Yeah, so I walked into the house, grabbed a knife,
and put it to his neck. I was going to kill him," she said.

"The only reason I didn't was because this foo' had no
fight in him.

He knew I was right and he needed to accept what was
coming."

"What did you do then?" I asked

"I went to go tell my mama, and instead she kicked

us out," she said, beginning to sob.

"Man…"

"I never felt safe with them. Never felt love.
The first time I ever felt love was having y'all,
and so I knew I had to get clean because I knew
I would never let anybody hurt my babies
in the same way my mama hurt me."

"That's why we ended up on the North Side?"

"That's how it started, but first I had to give y'all up to
foster care."

"WHAT?"

"Yeah, you don't remember? I guess you was only three."

I did remember then.

I just had forgotten.

"Did we all stay together?" I asked.

"No, they split y'all up, the two oldest with one family,
the two youngest with another on the North Side
while I was at the detox center and yo' dad was in prison.
It was the hardest thing I have ever had to do."

"Was I with a white couple?" I finally asked.

"Yep."

"I remember them looking over me
smiling when I woke up," I confessed.

"When I got clean and got my babies back,
I refused to go back to the South Side.
I met a friend that knew of a spot I could afford
and offered me work, so I stayed. But that brought on

its own problems, not just being one of the only black
families
over there, but you know, everything with yo' dad.
But the truth is, one of the reasons
I let yo' dad stay around for so long
is because I didn't trust a new man around y'all."

I had a lot

running through

my mind.

She stood up to

grab a tissue

as I let it all settle.

She came back

and sat down,

dry eyed

but sniffly.

"So, keep going, Ev. We have come a long way."

A knock on the door came.

"Oh boy, you got me over here talking.
Can you get that and tell them I will be right down?"
she said, running up the stairs.

"Yeah, but who is it?" I asked,
making my way to the door.

I opened to see a tall, dark-skinned

man with a small, neat afro,

thick prescription glasses,
a blue sports coat, and slacks.

Far from an

ordinary look on

the South Side.

Frankie introduced

himself and gently

asked for my mama.

I saw why

the chicken was

defrosting in the sink.

I called Michele

on my way home.

She was back

in Chico, completing

her final year.

Just an hour away,

so we spent most

weekends together.

I told her

about my day.

Being done

with football.

Even some of

what my mama

had revealed.

Looking back now,

I can point to

that call as a time

when I began

to slowly open

up to her.

To: Jackson (37)

That summer,

me, Tony, and Roger
got ourselves a

three-bedroom

in Davis. Which

meant I

switched roles

with Roger,

commuting 20

minutes one-way

to Sacramento.

That time of

the year,

UC students

faithfully cruised

the bike trails with

lighter-than-usual

loads in their book bags.

Roger got

me a job at

a vitamin store

he'd been working

at for the past year

before disappearing

from school for

a few months.

That's a topic

for another time.

Though before

he left and when

he returned,

life was good.
For living on Lake Boulevard,
we got full access

to Stonegate Country Club,
just by adding

five dollars a month onto our rent.

The club had tennis,
basketball courts,

a fitness center,

a club house,

and picnic areas.

Me, Roger, and

Tony frequently

launched the

canoes off

the club dock for

unintentional

romantic rides

on the manmade lake.

Though Michele

was too cautious
to join me, Roger

and Tony damn sure

used the canoes

to heighten
their chances
on first dates.

The following

summer was best
whenever our sweaty bodies

weren't stuck to our leather couch.

We took an anthropology

course together at the local

community college Tony attended.

When we got home,

a jog to the club

was next.

Forty-five minutes in

the fitness center,

however long it took

for one of us

to win a tennis match.

Then came

a dive in the pool.

Jog back home.

Dive in our

complex's pool—

stay in

most of the day

if not scheduled

to work.

Tony worked

at a popular bar

downtown, which

meant he always

got to swim longest.

If we were all off,
a day in the pool
would lead

to a night out.

To: Jackson (38)

Frankie privately proposed

to my mama, giving her

the only thing he had from

his deceased mama,

her wedding ring.

He moved into her spot
on the South Side,

then the recession hit,
and his construction jobs stopped.

Michele began working at

a public relations agency

in San Francisco,

sharing a three-bedroom flat

with college friends.

I was now

personal training

at a local gym.

I went with

Michele to

her long-time

friend's wedding,

at the country club

back home

on the North Side.

Her parents

were invited as well,
so I drove over with them.

The place

was surrounded

by crimson and gold

vineyards.

Michele and the eight

bridesmaids'

taupe dresses

paired well

with the November

weather and rustic venue.

I'd been to three weddings

before this.

All three had

not one

white person.

Two of them

I danced

until I sweat.

One, I hid

my tears

as my auntie
walked down the aisle.

I was
the only black person
at this one.

I'd mastered the ability
to stay on high alert
in the midst of fun.

Especially going out
with Michele's friends,
knowing a group of guys
could take advantage
of me being the

only guy in this

group full of women.

At a wedding,

I figured it was ok
to drop some
of the guard.

I drank

the free alcohol

that night.

Two drinks
I ordered with

Michele's dad

was all it took
to get me dancing.

The brown poison in

the clear glass matched

my button-down shirt.

I noticed Michele

on the wraparound deck
talking with Katie,

a girl we knew in school.

Remember her?

She was my

younger brother's age:

short, bleached-blonde hair,

prominent chest.

I walked out,

heard Katie talk

about her husband (one of the

groomsmen) and their new baby.

I grabbed a chair

as we spoke

about my niece

Jackie and my other

young nephew and nieces.

Michele spoke

with pride as she'd

spent time with the kids,
watching movies, taking
pumpkin-patch trips.

I could tell

she was thinking

of our future children

as well.

The alcohol

worked as an extra layer

for all standing

on the deck
that cold November.

I then felt

extra body heat nearby.

I looked up,

noticed a bald,

middle-aged white man

staring down on me.

"If you keep bumping into me, we are going to have a
problem," he said.

"What?" I said, jumping up, knowing I was in a vulnerable
position.

I noticed his

gray suit jacket

was open,

as if he had

prepared for

the moment.

He stepped closer,

less than an inch from
planting a kiss on my lips.

"I said if you keep bumping into me, we're going to have a
problem."

Do you remember
years ago,
we were with

my younger brother
at the complex,
our neighbor Hector
faked as if he were
about to hit him?

Do you remember

how many times

my brother hit him

before Hector

knew what happened?

Well, I didn't do that,
though those instincts

are far from dormant.

Instead, out of respect

for the bride and groom,
I shoved him away

to create space.

The next thing

I knew, he was being

pulled off me.

Michele had fallen
in the mix up,

I saw no blood,
felt no pain,
just hot rage.

I searched

for the man

as I hauled myself

to my feet.

I shouted

as if a wedding

never existed,

though

my target

was not in sight.

A middle-aged,

white-haired woman
in a black gown

grabbed my face.

"You son of a bitch, you ruined my nephew's wedding,"
she said, shaking my face.

Katie beat everyone
to stop her

by slamming her fist

into the lady's mouth.

Then came a short, pale man
with pointy ears, who

resembled the groom,

wrapping his arms

around my waist

in a pathetic

tackle attempt.

"What are you doing, Uncle Mike? This isn't his fault,"
the groom said, snatching him away.

Katie grabbed Michele,

instructed her husband
to grab me.

Katie drove us
through the darkened,

winding roads,

frantic,

intoxicated.

"Oh, I wish we would have let Andy get his ass kicked,"
Katie shouted.

Michele cried

next to me
in the back seat.

Katie's husband
remained calm
in the passenger seat.

"Take me back right now," I shouted.

"Fuck Andy, he isn't even worth it," her husband said
gently.

"No, I am going to get him," I insisted.

"He will get his someday, no matter what," he said.

"Wait, who is Andy?" I finally asked.

"He is the son of the guy that got in your face," Katie said.

The stepbrother of the bride.

"What about him? I asked.

"He stood on the side so you couldn't see him
and when you pushed his dad away from you,
he sucker punched you
and they both jumped on you
before I pulled them off," Katie's husband said.

"They have been doing that around bars on the North
Side," Katie said.
"When a black guy shows up from the South Side,
they wait until he gets drunk, follow him to the bathroom,

and beat him up. They are fucking scumbags."

The windows were up
to keep heat in the car.

I tried to break them
to get out.

They dropped us off

at Michele's parents.

I escaped,

walked up, and down

the Hawkings neighborhood,

making calls
to my sister,

my brothers,

Roger, Good,

Tony, my mama.

Perhaps I

never really
was in search of

blood because

I never reached out to you.

I never got my revenge.

Nor did I find solace

when I heard months later

that this Andy guy
was beaten half to death

by a brotha he and his dad
jumped before.

INT. THERAPIST'S OFFICE – DAY – MID JUNE 2015

Evan is seated in his usual spot on the couch.

EVAN:

I've haven't heard from Jack in some time, I feel uneasy about it.

THERAPIST:

Why uneasy?

EVAN:

At first, I was thinking I pissed him off because while I am writing about my future and being a college kid, his uncle Stevie was killed around that time. But now I think it's because he is tired of reading about me and Michele's relationship. I did steal her from him.

THERAPIST:

From what I am reading, it sounds like you're doing what you initially wanted to do.

EVAN:

Yeah—well, maybe I need to try something else.

THERAPIST:

Like what?

EVAN:

I don't know. But my life is pretty predictable.

THERAPIST:

Is that how you see it?

EVAN:

Yes, well, it's predictable that the unpredictable will happen. I don't know. But there's definitely a pattern.

THERAPIST:

Tell me about those next few years then.

EVAN:

Uh, let me think. My mom's fiancé Frankie got depressed after losing work and refused help, and then, like my dad, seemed to start getting sick as soon as my mama was ready to move on.

THERAPIST:

Was he really sick?

EVAN:

A lot of people in my family didn't believe it. No one really liked him after a while, so I don't know.

Uh, my younger brother gave up football after trying to get on with a pro team and started working as a personal trainer.

I eventually left the gym and got a job working for a recruiting agency in the financial district.

Umm, then me and Michele moved in together in San Francisco.

THERAPIST:

How was the transition living together after not living in the same town for so long?

EVAN:

Living together was great. The neighborhood was beautiful, right near the water and great restaurants.

THERAPIST:

Oh, that's right, I remember you talking about the people.

EVAN:

Yeah, this was like a neighborhood full of the preppy kids I used to go to school with. So, of course, I never felt comfortable. To the point that I usually left the neighborhood if I wanted to do anything more than pick up food.

THERAPIST:

Did you know you'd feel this way before moving?

EVAN:

Oh yeah, I made it clear I did not want to live in that area, but most of Michele's friends lived there and she wanted to remain close. I wanted her to have that. Plus, I was transitioning into my new job working 70 hours a week. I really didn't have much energy to care, you know?

THERAPIST:

Yes, and I can also see how conflicted you must have been. You had worked hard to be in a nice environment— and then when you get there, you don't connect with the people.

EVAN:

Exactly. When my mama came to visit, she was in awe of where we lived, so I found it hard to complain about living in this beautiful and safe area with rent control when she was still on the South Side.

THERAPIST:

That makes sense.

EVAN:

But I didn't last a year at the new job. I started working at an accounting firm Michele's college friend helped me get. And then I decided to go back to school.

THERAPIST:

Ok, so as I recall, you went to get your master's and started coaching football at the local junior college, what else?

EVAN:

Yep, kept a full-time job at the accounting firm then obviously, I ran myself down trying to balance two full-time jobs and grad school. So I gave up the stability of the accounting firm.

THERAPIST:

Is this the pattern you are referring to?

EVAN:

Yeah, every time I worked toward a goal, either something challenging happened or I left it, and then had to crawl my way back up to do something else.

THERAPIST:

I see that too, but would it be a bit more accurate to say
that you had found a way to do, but not feel?

EVAN:

…

THERAPIST:

…

EVAN:

Yes…

THERAPIST:

A lot has happened in your life, Evan. I am curious just
how often you think you allow yourself to feel your
feelings?

EVAN:

Not very often.

THERAPIST:

…

EVAN:

Do you think Jack can see through this, too?

THERAPIST:

I think Jack is hurt. He doesn't trust you, but through all of these years, I get the feeling that he loves you unlike any friend you have ever had. How many friends do you know would stick around after all that has happened between you?

EVAN:

None. So, what do you suggest I do?

THERAPIST:

Let me ask you something. Why do you think you started talking to him about the day your mother died?

EVAN:

I don't know, it's just what came up.

THERAPIST:

Ok, so why not go back to that time again? I know its fresh, but see how that feels, because as we both know, this is the event that brought you to your knees.

Being attacked

at the wedding

changed my relationship

with Michele.

Thoughts of

this never happening

had I stuck to the

plan of marrying

Clair Huxtable

became relentless.

That's when

I started to tell her
about my difficulties
with finding peace.

In some

white neighborhoods,

I could be

considered a criminal.

In some

black neighborhoods,

I could be

misidentified as

a rival.

I told her how when my dad

was a teenager in New York,

some guy walked up to him,
opened his coat,
put a sawn-off shotgun

to his chest, then said,

"Oh, wrong one,"

and walked off.

I also told

her of a time
I was visited

by a private detective

at the gym

I worked for.

He pulled a surveillance picture
out of a manila folder,

asked if the black man

in the picture,
who had long dreads
and was twenty years my senior,

was me.

I know you

would have spoken
about these things

with her
from the jump.

I'd gotten fixated

on becoming someone
of significance.
Someone to do

heavy lifting

so those I love

could find

their way.

Initially noble,

one could say,

in the end naïve.

Michele knew

she could never

fully understand.

Subtle changes came.

As I shared more,

she learned

I couldn't move

through life

the same way

her friends and their

significant others did.

~

I proposed to

Michele on

our trip to

the central coast.

I had been saving money

for a ring,

then collaborated

with Michele's sister
to figure out
what she would like.

Bought one and hid it well,

like a young hobbit.

Please know

I am not writing this

to hurt you,

only to give context
for what transpired

leading up to

the most difficult

day of my life.

Michele's aunts

organized the

engagement party.

My mama

brought Frankie,

who had seemed

to find his way

out of despair.

I didn't invite

my dad nor

was I planning to

invite him
to the wedding.

~

I received a

4.0 in my

first semester

of graduate

school.

All was well

until it wasn't.

Pains of the

past began to

creep up.

A co-worker

at my old accounting firm

had mentioned
his therapist
a while back.

I reached out
for more information.

It was Christmas break
after my first year
coaching at the college.

I had time off

for my master's program, too—

and I finally made the call.

~

My therapist recently shared
that, prior to seeing me,
a longtime client
lost her life to a

heinous crime.

Said the

only gift gained

was becoming

more equipped

to support me.

Likewise, my experiences
with our friend Roger

help me.

When I talk to

Roger today, we

speak of
our time in Davis

with deep reverence.

Yet we also

talk about how

he disappeared

for three months

before returning

back that summer.

How he was diagnosed

with manic depression

and bipolar disorder.

Listening to him
gave me insight
on a struggle

we all still know

little about.

How mental illness manifests

in different people,

especially when they

don't receive

the proper help.

Evan returns to the story of his mother's death.

To: Jackson (40)

"Is it true?" I interrogated my older brother who called

me from the police station just as I got off
the phone with my sister.

"She gon' man. That nigga shot her."

The roar

built from

my stomach.

I'm sure
it shook
the car
and no doubt

Tony, who drove
as I received
this news.

I spiked my phone

on the front

passenger seat floor.

I lost track of time after that.

When we

pulled up
to my mama's

place on the South Side,
I was unbuckled,

hanging out

the car before

we came to a stop.

Police cars

flooded the street.

Yellow caution tape

snaked around

the townhouse.

Tony stayed in his car.

The haze in the air
seemed to have followed us
from the city.

My younger brother
sat on a brick bench

on the front lawn
as his girlfriend

rubbed his back.

I ducked

under the yellow tape,

ran toward the front door,
ready to kill him
before they took his ass

to jail.

I was intercepted

by two officers

who assured me

Frankie had already

taken his own life.

I turned around,

walked to

the front lawn,

dropped

to my knees—

punishing

the earth

with swift blows.

In that kind of

grief, it's easy

to go from

completely distraught

to disbelieving
in a moment.

My older

brother and

his girlfriend returned

from the police

station after answering

questions about

how they had

found the bodies.

"We were knocking for a while and the doors

were locked, but I heard a pop sound
come from upstairs. So I kicked the door in,
saw her on the living room floor, next to the couch.
Then I ran upstairs and found him…"

My brother saw

Frankie's eyes
were rolled backward

after a shot he put

in his own neck.

I told them Mama had

called me a few weeks before,
telling me she was giving Frankie

a thirty days' notice,
said they hadn't been

a couple for some time,
that she was

sleeping on her couch.

I told them

I hadn't paid

it any mind.

I'd invited her

and my younger brother

to help pick out

tuxedos with

me and Michele,

as our wedding was just
two months away.

The police

were certain

he shot her

days before

while she slept

on her couch

before killing himself

that day.

Which explained

why we couldn't

reach her.

My sister

had been

in Southern

California for

Jackie's cheer

competition

when she

called me.

In a panic,

as she waited

for a flight home,

my sister

wrote out

a post on

social media

asking for help.

This reached

Michele's sister
who called her.

Later, I looked

down the street,

noticed Roger,

who saw

the post also,

walking over.

He was trying

to get on his feet

after another

manic episode,
living back home

on the East Side

with his parents.

He was no longer

a small hibernating bear.

Now his stomach

and face were swollen
from his medication.

I could see
from a distance

his face was red,

his hands trembling.

By the time we embraced,
he was crying more

than I had ever

seen him cry before.

Michele pulled

up after a friend

dropped her off.

We left before
the bodies
were taken out.

~

Tears, however painful,
create the valleys
we need
to hold joy.

In the next days,
we retold stories,
laughing at things
most would find horrific.

We had to.

Our laughter

ended when

it was time

to go home—

forcing us to face
our new reality.

Though receiving no response, Evan keeps writing.

To: Jackson (41)

The funeral was held

at Faith Baptist Church

on the South Side.

The church was packed

with faces that resembled
every area of the city.

We celebrated

in our funeral attire

back at my older brother's place.

I listened in

to a conversation

my younger brother
had with Michele,

telling her how much
he'd always

admired me.

My older brother

pulled me aside

directly telling me

the same thing.

Their words

validated

I had become

the man

I'd set out to be.

Why did

I not feel it?

~

I returned
to coaching, completed

my master's program,

started teaching

at the college.

The need

to push forward

still lived on.

~

Me and Michele

were married that spring—

to avoid conflict

with football season.

The venue was

an art and wine exhibit

nestled in a vineyard.

Red, white, and orange flowers

surrounded the property

as did olive trees
with extravagant paintings

hanging from their limbs.

A rustic barn held

cocktail hour,

later a dance floor.

I placed a single rose
on an empty chair
in the front row
for my mama.

Michele's veil

swayed with

the wind.

Etta James' "At Last"
played as rays of love
beamed from her eyes.

After a kiss, a cry,

and our "I do's",

the guests

were escorted

to the cocktail area.

I hid near a pond
to be alone,

waited until Michele
switched out of her dress

for cocktail hour
to show my face.

~

The next year

was tough

on us both.

Not because

we didn't want

to be married.

Michele had

to balance her own grief
while attending

to me.

She also had to
get to know this person
who was no longer the one

she planned to marry
when she said yes.

Coaching football
had lost its thrill.

I had gone

through jobs,

experienced many things

I'd only dreamed of.
Now I had
no other place

to hide.

We worked out

my struggles
in therapy. Then

one day in January,

I walked

in for my session

and told my therapist
I wanted to talk

more about you.

For if I was

going to truly heal,
I would have to address

why I pulled away
and tried to forget you.

From: Jackson (42)

So now what?

Are we finished

again?

Have you gotten

what you wanted

out of this?

To: Jackson (43)

No…

Not just yet.

I've felt strange

referring to her as

Mama while writing

to you, knowing

growing up

we only called her
Trese.

We heard it

from the family

when we lived

with Grandmomma

and she thought

it was too cute to correct.

When I stepped

away from coaching,

I had space
to work through

some of the past.

Michele says

it's like I've had

two lives—

Being caught

stealing with Marcel,

running around

the South Side

trying to be

a thug.

Then Trese

sitting us down

for an intervention.

I told Michele

that was the moment

I was no longer

Jackson.

She told me,

though she didn't know

all of Jackson's story,
she saw him come out

from time to time
whenever we talked.

She had always

seen you—

which is to

say—

seen me.

You knew

she had.

I tried to hide it.

I can see now

the shame

of being oneself,

does not compare

to the shame of losing
oneself.

From: Jackson (44)

Then why

did you leave?

Why did you

take me away

from writing?

Why did you

force me

to hide

my anger?

Or treat me

like I was

bad?

Why did you put me
in places I didn't

feel comfortable

being?

Make me act

as if I am

more outgoing

than I am?

I used to
love sports when
we played for fun.

Why did you
make me play
when I didn't
want to anymore?

Why did you
keep me from
Michele? When
she wanted to
get to know more
about me?

You don't
have any
answers, do you?

This was all
so you don't
feel guilty.

That's why I
don't trust you.

INT. THERAPIST'S OFFICE — DAY — JULY 2015

THERAPIST:

How are you feeling?

EVAN:

Terrible.

THERAPIST:

…

EVAN:

…

THERAPIST:

…

EVAN:

…Yeah, I don't know what else there is to say about it.

THERAPIST:

That's ok.

EVAN:

…

THERAPIST:

We have been working together for a couple of years now and most of it has been dealing with your mother's death. But I can tell you that I have learned a lot more about you through this. You have been extremely open, which makes my job easier.

EVAN:

…

THERAPIST:

You know, when you came to our session this past January and told me what you wanted to do, I immediately thought about a time my sister went on a retreat years ago where she had to do a writing exercise with her dominant and non-dominant hand. She said as she did it, she noticed when using her dominant hand, her writing voice was familiar, but when she used her non-dominant hand, a different voice emerged. She called it her inner child.

EVAN:

(Nods)

THERAPIST:

I didn't want to set any parameters for how you should go about connecting with yours because it's possible what she did wouldn't work for you. But I thought it was a great idea that you started texting and then emailing yourself.

EVAN:

Yeah.

THERAPIST:

You know, at some level, all of us grow up having to shove a part of our full self down and put on a mask as a protection from hurt.

But you had to do this to literally survive. Of course, we can't get rid of our inner child. Jack showed up even as you got older and you tried to squelch him by staying super busy.

But I hope you show yourself some grace. To be a black boy growing up how you did in that environment is challenging enough, but then you are also a highly sensitive soul, which heightens the pain. It's a miracle you are where you are today.

You look like you have something to say, Evan. What's on your mind?

EVAN:

I am thinking about Jack or uh, little me, and all that I made him do. But each time, it got to a place where he couldn't take it anymore. Like when I walked away from football that first time I was at Butte. It was a mystery then, but if I looked closer then, I would have known I just didn't want to play.

THERAPIST:

You are right, but you needed it as a kid.

EVAN:

Yeah.

THERAPIST:

I also want to point out that when your mom sat you down after stealing with your cousin, she was doing all she could to guide you in the right direction. But she was also asking you to figure out how you wanted to live your life when you were far too young to know.

So all your little brain could comprehend was "I am bad as I am." When really, you mimicked what you saw around you and instead of being seen as a boy crying out for help, you were seen as bad. Think about it, you got harassed when you leaned into being "Mr. Do-right Evan." How do you think it would have turned out for you by strictly being Jackson?

EVAN:

Not good. That's why I started to idealize the future I wanted. Which led to my falling in love with the idea of people instead of real people, including Michele.

THERAPIST:

It's a good thing Michele has always seen you. Which is to say she's seen through the front you put up. Because it's clear you love her. Idealizing was just your tactic to survive. And as you already know, you had yourself a great mama alongside of you to make sure that you did survive—and thrive.

EVAN:

But Jackson—little me is still mad.

THERAPIST:

Of course he is, he has been abandoned. So it's your job now that you are an adult to gain his trust.

EVAN:

How do I gain his trust?

THERAPIST:

You have to tell the little you inside that you were just a kid yourself when you needed protection. And you tried to change the way you lived in order to protect yourself from harm. But again, you were just a kid.

Now that you are an adult, you can be there for your inner child in a way you weren't able to be before.

EVAN:

I understand.

THERAPIST:

It will take some time, but start with that and continue to write and see what comes up. And like any other relationship, trust will build over time. It's worth nurturing this relationship because we lose things when we abandon our inner child.

EVAN:

Like what?

THERAPIST:

Like our natural talents and authentic zest for life. In your dad's case, his abandoned inner child lost him a relationship with you. Could you imagine how different things would have turned out had he known this? So yes, you were going down a dangerous path, but Jack also has the heart of an artist, which was lost.

EVAN:

(sighs)

THERAPIST:

I am looking forward to getting to know the whole you.

To: Jackson (45)

A story that pops up
for me is one you told

about the school barbecue.

When those parents
got on you about

getting into fights
with their kids,
I keep feeling

it would have

been nice

to have Trese

or our pops

there, huh?

To feel safe.

It would

have been

nice if

I could

have been

there for

you, too.

But I couldn't

then, because

I was just

a kid, too—

I didn't know

how to parent

us, and I

am sorry

you suffered

because of it.

I really am.

Life has a way
of doing for you
what you

won't do for

yourself.

Which has

put me in

this position,

as an adult,

to be able

to be here

for you now.

To listen

to your

needs.

To feel

all of the

pain you feel.

I know it

is scary.

But I am

here, and

it is my

dying promise

when I say

that I will

never leave

us again.

You have always

loved words.

So I know

you understand

that some words

carry more weight

than others.

Sometimes

no matter the

effort, words

can never do.

For it is only

action over

time that can

develop a

bond.

So I will

try this—

I am closing

my eyes as

I write you—

Let's imagine

sitting on

that bench

as a kid,

watching

the other kids
and their families

eating together.

What do you feel?

From: Jackson (46)

Alone.

Mad.

Confused.

Sad.

I even feel

hate.

Why them,

and not me?

I look

around at their

skin, then at mine,

and wonder

is it this?

I look

down at my

dirty shoes

and wonder

is it this?

Then realize

my skin

had something

to do with
why our family
didn't have money
for new shoes.

Jackson Evan Harris weeps.

To: Jackson (47)

My eyes are

closed again—

Would it

be ok if

I come over

and sit down

on the bench

and eat

lunch with

you?

From: Jackson (48)

Ok.

To: Jackson (49)

It feels really nice
to sit with you.

How do

you feel?

From: Jackson (50)

Good. Better.

To: Jackson (51)

Can I give

you a hug?

From: Jackson (52)

Yes.

To: Jackson (53)

How would it feel
if I come sit with you
every day?

Maybe we can

write stories?

Play basketball?

I have to

do adult

things, too,

but I won't

leave you

like I did before.

From: Jackson (54)

That would

be nice.

To: Jackson (55)

Ok, that's

great to hear.

I want to share
another story
with you.

When you asked

me why
I was reaching out
to you,

it is true

part of the reason

had to do with Trese

dying.

But something else
happened in January
that is really
responsible

for this.

INT. THERAPIST'S OFFICE — DAY — LATE
JULY 2015

Fade out.

A small brick building sits on a charming off street some place in Northern California. Inside is a rented office space, but what was never on display throughout this story is an oatmeal-colored armchair, a wooden bookshelf, one round end table, a lamp, and a psychotherapist.

What is on display is a black-framed MFT degree from Cal State East Bay, one round end table holding a black potted peace lily. One green leather couch, holding one of our main characters Jackson Evan Harris 6'0-6'1, slender, but lean, dark brown complexion, an unkempt afro, a beard, not so neat and patchy.

He reads to his therapist the most recent message he sent.

To: Jackson (56)

It was early

January 2015.

The sun

was already

shooting through our

large San Francisco

apartment windows.

Michele was

on her laptop,

in our living room,

looking at listings

for apartments

in other

neighborhoods.

She was packed,

waiting for me

to finish before

we set off

on our now

annual trip

to the central

coast.

"Ok, I'm done," I said, walking out of our single bedroom.

"I need to use the restroom before we go," Michele said.

I stared out of

the windows—

looking into

our neighbors'

maintained

garden and pond.

The bathroom

door opened.

"Hey, babe, can you come here for a second?" Michele
said with concern.

"Look at this—" she continued.

Two red lines

appeared
on a white stick.

My eyes went

to hers.

I had always

wanted this.

Though the year

after Trese

died made

me cynical—

For the first time

forcing thoughts like:

"How could I
bring a child

into a world

like this?"

Thankfully

in the last

year, the

beauty of

new life

was restored.

We hadn't

planned it—

but we were not
not trying.

Michele watched me close

to read my reaction.

She softened

when she saw

my joy.

On the drive,
I started to feel
the responsibility

of it.

One major

responsibility

in particular.

For I then knew

that in order

to love this child
in the way

she or he deserved

to be loved,

I had better

start loving

you first.

ACKNOWLEDGEMENTS

I am beyond grateful for all my guides and teachers along the way, for your protection, knowledge and wisdom. For TIP who told me during one of our sessions, "Oh, you HAVE to write this book," which was the extra boost I needed. With your support, a cycle has been broken in my family. To Leslie Crane, this book's first editor. I still remember the dinner we all had at House of Prime Rib after another round of revisions back in 2015. I appreciate your patience with a then new writer. Years later, I made major revisions and experimented with form, so I want to say thank you, Lanette Sweeney, for taking on such project and pushing me to make difficult decisions to bring clarity to my vision. Thank you, Asante Simons for putting your final touches on this project. Thank you, Rebecca Ruger for your beautiful cover design. Big thanks to the writers in my life for your advice and friendship. Thank you to all my beta readers and the ones who have yet to read this book but have been patiently waiting all these years. B—I appreciate you always sending positive words my way whenever you ask about my writing. Flo—I appreciate our Friday mid-morning drives around the city and our late-night walk through Manhattan as I told you about this project. Thanks to anyone who decides to read this book. May you reconnect with your truest best friend you might have lost touch with over the years.

To my amazing family. Glo, thank you for all the praise after you finished reading this story. Your approval was more important to me then you will ever know. To my niece, Teia, for your seal of approval, yet that would never surpass your approval of me as your uncle. To Kendrick, you were in your mama's belly as I stayed up late writing this book. Outside of writing, the work needed to be done addressing past wounds was the most difficult thing I ever had to do and, without the thought of you coming into this world, I may not have been able to go through with it. Thank you and your little brother for giving me the best title ever. Not Author, but Your Dad. Thanks to those who have no idea what I am doing with this writing thing yet have always remained kind. To my mama, I miss you every day. I will never be able to scribble down enough words to express that fully. And to Dana, you were right next to me when I woke up with this idea. You were right next to me when I typed the final word of the book. You have been right next to me all these years and there is no one I would rather have by my side navigating this crazy, and beautiful world.